I0622034

THE FIRE-FLY'S LOVERS

Also from Westphalia Press

westphaliapress.org

THE FIRE-FLY'S LOVERS

AND OTHER FAIRY TALES OF OLD JAPAN

BY WILLIAM ELLIOT GRIFFIS

WESTPHALIA PRESS
AN IMPRINT OF POLICY STUDIES ORGANIZATION

THE FIRE-FLY'S LOVERS AND OTHER FAIRY TALES FROM OLD JAPAN
ALL RIGHTS RESERVED © 2015 BY POLICY STUDIES ORGANIZATION

WESTPHALIA PRESS
AN IMPRINT OF POLICY STUDIES ORGANIZATION
1527 NEW HAMPSHIRE AVE., NW
WASHINGTON, D.C. 20036
INFO@IPSONET.ORG

ISBN-13: 978-1941472873
ISBN-10: 1941472877

COVER DESIGN BY TAILLEFER LONG AT ILLUMINATED STORIES:
WWW.ILLUMINATEDSTORIES.COM

DANIEL GUTIERREZ-SANDOVAL, EXECUTIVE DIRECTOR
PSO AND WESTPHALIA PRESS

UPDATED MATERIAL AND COMMENTS ON THIS EDITION
CAN BE FOUND AT THE WESTPHALIA PRESS WEBSITE:
WWW.WESTPHALIAPRESS.ORG

THE FIRE-FLY'S LOVERS

AND OTHER FAIRY TALES OF OLD JAPAN

WILLIAM ELLIOT GRIFFIS

To my classmate
ROBERT CLARENCE PRUYN
who in student days opened
for me the jewelled gates of
JAPANESE   FAIRY-LAND

"OPEN SESAME"

IN the old feudal days of Japan, a knight or
gentleman riding on horseback within city
limits was always preceded by a groom,
who ran ahead and shouted to the people to get
out of the way, warning the children at play,
lifting the babies out of danger, and thus making
a clear track for the rider who followed him.
His bare back was tattooed with wonderful
figures of heroes, dragons and the many strange
creatures that dwell in fairy-land. Indeed,
when I lived in Japan I was first attracted into
the wonder-world of the people by studying the
legends and marvels thus pictured on human
skin. Thence I went to the flower shows and
tableaux, by which, in living blooms and in-
geniously blended colors, the florists of Nippon
set forth the national lore. My studies were
more advanced and my delight greater when, in
the art and language, new doors were opened
into the treasure chambers of "The Country
Between Heaven and Earth."

The stories in this little volume are the direct
result of what I saw and studied through these
inviting doors. Some were suggested by native

custom, and artists' pictures, while others were spun from my own brain. But all of them, I feel sure, reflect the spirit of Old Japan. "The Fire-Fly's Lovers," "The Child of the Thunder," "Little Silver's Dream," "Lord Cuttle-Fish's Concert," "Lord Long-Legs' Procession," and "The Gift of Gold Lacquer," exist in no Japanese text. They were suggested by what I saw of the lovely, the comic, or the pompous side of life in a Daimio's Castle. Several of the others have been adapted from native legends and operas. Such old friends as "The Tongue-Cut Sparrow," "The Ape and the Crab," "The Two Frogs," and "The Idol and the Whale," are partly folk-lore, and partly of definite authorship.

As for the Japanese names and phrases, I think you will have no trouble with them, if you will remember that *a* is pronounced as in father, *ai* as in aisle, *e* as in prey, *ei* as in weigh, *o* as in bore, and *u* as in rule, or as in boot. Thus, Fukui sounds as if spelled Foo-koo-ee, Benkei as Benkay, Rai as rye, etc.

So, "*o idé nasari*" (please, honorable one, enter) as they say in Japan.

W. E. G.

Ithaca, N. Y., April, 1908.

CONTENTS

Princess Fire-Fly is put in prison.

ILLUSTRATIONS

THE FIRE-FLY'S LOVERS

THE FIRE-FLY'S LOVERS

O N the southern and sunny side of the castle moats of the Fukui castle, in Echizen, the water had long ago become shallow so that lotus lilies grew luxuriantly. Deep in the heart of one of the great flowers whose petals were as pink as the lining of a sea-shell, lived the King of the Fire-Flies, Hi-ō, whose only daughter was the lovely Princess Hotaru. While still a child the Princess had been carefully kept at home within the pink petals of the lily, never going even to the edges except to see her father fly off on his journey. Dutifully she waited until of age, when the fire glowed in her own body, and shone, beautifully illuminating the lotus, until its light gleamed like a lamp within a globe of coral.

Every night her light grew brighter and brighter, until at last it was as mellow as gold. Then her father said :

"My daughter is now of age, she may fly abroad with me sometimes, and when the proper suitor comes she may marry whom she will."

3

So Hotaru flew forth in and out among the lotus lilies of the moat, then into rich rice fields, and at last far off to the indigo meadows.

Wherever she went a crowd of suitors followed her, for she had the singular power of attracting all the night-flying insects to herself. But she cared for none of their attentions, and though she spoke politely to them all she gave encouragement to none. Yet some of the sheeny-winged gallants called her a coquette.

One night she said to her mother, the Queen :

"I have met many admirers, but I do not wish a husband from any of them. To-night I shall stay at home, and if any of them love me truly they will come and pay me court here. Then I shall lay an impossible duty on them. If they are wise they will not try to perform it ; but if they love their lives more than they love me, I do not want any of them. Whoever succeeds may have me for his bride."

"As you will, my child," said the Queen-mother, who arrayed her daughter in her most resplendent robes, and set her on her throne in the heart of the lotus.

Then she gave orders to her body-guard to keep all suitors at a respectful distance lest some stupid gallant, a Horn-bug or a Cockchafer dazzled by the light, should approach too near and hurt the Princess or shake her throne.

No sooner had twilight faded away, than forth came the Golden Beetle, who stood on a stamen and making obeisance, said : —

" I am Lord Green-Gold. I offer my house, my fortune, and my love to Princess Hotaru."

" Go and bring me fire and I will be your bride," said Hotaru.

With a bow of the head the beetle opened his wings and departed with a stately whirr.

Next came a shining bug with wings and body as black as lamp-smoke, who solemnly professed his passion. He received the same answer :

" Bring me fire, and you may have me for your wife."

Off flew the bug with a buzz.

Pretty soon came the scarlet Dragon-fly, expecting so to dazzle the Princess by his gorgeous colors that she would accept him at once.

" I decline your offer," said the Princess, " unless you bring me a flash of fire."

Swift was the flight of the Dragon-fly on his errand, and in came the Beetle with a tremendous buzz, and ardently pleaded his suit.

"I will say 'yes' if you bring me fire," said the glittering Princess.

Suitor after suitor appeared to woo the daughter of the King of the Fire-Flies until every petal was dotted with them. One after another in a long troop they appeared. Each in his own way, proudly, humbly, boldly, mildly, with flattery, with boasting, even with tears, proffered his love, told his rank or expatiated on his fortune or vowed his constancy, sang his tune or played his music. To every one of her lovers the Princess in modest voice returned the same answer:

"Bring me fire, and I'll be your bride."

So without telling his rivals, each one thinking he had the secret alone sped away after fire.

But none ever came back to wed the Princess. Alas for the poor suitors! The Beetle whizzed off to a house near by through the paper windows of which light glimmered. So full was he of his passion that thinking nothing of wood or iron, he dashed his head against a nail, and fell dead on the ground.

The black bug flew into a room where a poor student was reading. His lamp was only a dish of earthenware full of rape seed oil with a wick made of pith. Knowing nothing of oil the love-lorn bug crawled into the dish to reach the flame and in a few seconds was drowned as in a sea.

"What's that?" said a thrifty housewife, sitting with needle in hand, as her lamp flared up for a moment, smoking the chimney, and then cracking it; while picking out the scorched bits she found a roasted Dragon-Fly, whose scarlet wings were all burned off.

Mad with love the brilliant Hawk-Moth, afraid of the flame yet determined to win the fire for the Princess, hovered round and round the candle flame, coming nearer and nearer each time. "Now or never, the Princess or death," he buzzed, as he darted forward to snatch a flash of flame, but singeing his wings, he fell help-lessly down, and died in agony.

"What a fool he was, to be sure," said the ugly Clothes-Moth, coming on the spot. "I'll get the fire. I'll crawl up *inside* the candle." So he climbed up the hollow paper wick, and was nearly to the top, and close to the blue part of the flame, when the man, snuffing the wick, crushed him to death.

Sad indeed was the fate of the lovers of Hi-ō's daughter. Some hovered around the beacons on the headland, some fluttered about the great wax candles which stood eight feet high in their brass sockets in the temples of Buddha; some burned their noses at the top of incense sticks, or were nearly choked by the smoke; some danced all night around the lanterns in the shrines; some sought the sepulchral lamps in the graveyards; one visited the cremation furnace; another the kitchen, where a feast was going on; another chased the sparks that flew out of the chimney; but none brought fire to the Princess, or won the lover's prize. Many lost their feelers, had their shining bodies scorched or their wings singed, but most of them alas! lay dead, black and cold next morning.

As the priests trimmed the lamps in the shrines, and the servant maids the lanterns, each said alike:

"The Princess Hotaru must have had many lovers last night."

Alas! alas! poor suitors. Some tried to snatch a streak of green fire from the cat's eyes, and were snapped up for their pains. One attempted to get a mouthful of bird's breath, but was swallowed alive.   A Carrion-Beetle (the ugly lover) crawled off to the seashore, and found some fish scales that emitted light.   The Stag-Beetle climbed a mountain, and in a rotten tree stump found some bits of glowing wood like fire, but the distance was so great that long before they reached the castle moat it was daylight, and the fire had gone out ; so they threw their fish scales and old wood away.

The next day was one of great mourning, and there were so many funerals going on that Hi-marō the Prince of the Fire-Flies on the north side of the castle moat inquired of his servants the cause.   Then he learned for the first time of the glittering Princess.

Upon this the Prince, who had just succeeded his father upon the throne, fell in love with the Princess and resolved to marry her.   He sent his chamberlain to ask of her father his daughter in marriage according to true etiquette.   The father agreed to the Prince's proposal, with the condition that the Prince should obey her behest in one thing, which was to come in person bringing her fire.

Then the Prince at the head of his glittering battalions came in person and filled the lotus palace with a flood of golden light. But Hotaru was so beautiful that her charms paled not their fire even in the blaze of the Prince's glory. The visit ended in wooing, and the wooing in wedding. On the night appointed, in a palanquin made of the white lotus-petals, amid the blazing torches of the Prince's battallions of warriors, Hotaru was borne to the Prince's palace, and there Prince and Princess were joined in wedlock.

Many generations have passed since Hi-marō and Hotaru were married, and still it is the whim of all Fire-Fly princesses that their base-born lovers must bring fire as their love-offering or lose their prize. Else would the glittering fair ones be wearied unto death by the importunity of their lovers. Great indeed is the loss, for in this quest of fire many thousand insects, attracted by the Fire-Fly, are burned to death in the vain hope of winning the fire that shall gain the cruel but beautiful one that fascinates them. It is for this cause that each night insects hover around the lamp flame, and every morning a crowd of victims drowned in the oil, or scorched in the flame, must be cleaned from the lamp. This is the reason why young ladies catch and imprison the Fire-Flies to watch the war of insect-love, in the hope that they may have human lovers who will dare as much, through fire and flood, as they.

THE TRAVELS OF THE TWO FROGS

LONG, long ago, in the good old days before the hairy-faced and pale-cheeked men from over the Sea of Great Peace came to Japan; before the black coal-smoke and snorting iron horse scared the white heron from the rice-fields; before black crows and fighting sparrows, which fear not man, perched on telegraph wires, or ever a railway was thought of, there lived two Frogs—one in a well in Kioto, the other in a lotus-pond in Osaka, forty miles away.

Now it is a common proverb in the Land of the Gods[1] that "the frog in the well knows not the great ocean," and the Kioto Frog had so often heard this scornful sneer from the maids who came to draw out water, with their long bamboo-handled buckets that he resolved to travel abroad and see the world, and especially the great ocean.

"I'll see for myself," said Mr. Frog, as he packed his wallet and wiped his spectacles,

[1] Japan.

12

"what this great ocean is that they talk so much about. I'll wager it isn't half as deep or wide as my well, where I can see the stars even at daylight."

Now the truth was, a recent earthquake had greatly reduced the depth of the well and the water was getting very shallow. Mr. Frog informed the family of his intentions. Mrs. Frog wept a great deal; but, drying her eyes with her paper handkerchief, she declared she would count the hours on her fingers till he came back, and at every morning and evening meal would set out his table with food on it, just as if he were at home. She tied up a little lacquered box full of boiled rice and snails for his journey, wrapped it around with a silk napkin, and, putting his extra clothes in a bundle, swung it on his back. Tying it over his neck, he seized his staff and was ready to go.

"*Sayonara*," cried he, as, with a tear in his eye, he walked away; for that is the Japanese for "good-bye."

"*Sayonara*," croaked Mrs. Frog and the whole family of young frogs in a chorus.

Two of the tiniest froggies were still babies, that is, they were yet pollywogs, with a half inch of tail still on them ; and, of course, were carried about by being strapped on the back of their older brothers.

Mr. Frog being now on land, out of his well, noticed that the other animals did not leap, but walked upright on their hind legs ; and, not wishing to be eccentric, he likewise began briskly walking the same way.

Now it happened that about the same time the Osaka Frog had become restless and dissatisfied with life on the edges of his lotus-ditch. He had made up his mind to " cast the lion's cub into the valley."

" Why ! that *is* tall talk for a frog, I must say !" you may exclaim.   " What did he mean ?"

To see what he meant, we will go back a bit. I must tell you that the Osaka Frog was a philosopher.   Right at the edge of his lotus-pond was a monastery, full of Buddhist monks, who every day studied their sacred rolls and droned over the books of the sage, to learn them by heart.   Our frog had heard them so often that he could (in frog language, of course) repeat many of their wise sentences and intone responses to their evening prayers put up by the great idol Amida.   Indeed, our Frog had so often listened to their debates on texts from the classics that he had himself become a sage and a philosopher. Yet, as the proverb says, " the sage is not happy."

Why not? In spite of a soft mud-bank, plenty of green scum, stagnant water, and shady lotus leaves, a fat wife, and a numerous family— in short, everything to make a frog happy—his forehead, or rather gullet, was wrinkled with care from long pondering of knotty problems, such as the following :

The monks often came down to the edge of the pond to look at the pink and white lotus. One summer day, as a little frog, hardly out of his tadpole state, with a small fragment of tail still left, sat basking on a huge round leaf, one monk said to another :

" Of what does that remind you ? "

" The babies of frogs will become but frogs," said one shaven pate, laughing.

" What think you ? "

" The white lotus flower springs out of tho black mud," said the other, solemnly, as both walked away.

The old Frog, sitting near by, overheard them and began to philosophize : " Humph ! The babies of frogs will become but frogs, hey ? If mud becomes lotus, why shouldn't a frog become a man? Why not? If my pet son should travel abroad and see the world—go to Kioto, for instance—why shouldn't he be as wise as those shining-headed men, I wonder? I shall try it, anyhow. I'll send my son on a journey to Kioto. I'll ' cast the lion's cub into the valley,' " which, you see, meant pretty much the same thing.

Plump! splash! sounded the water, as a pair of webby feet disappeared. The "lion's cub" was soon ready, after much paternal advice, and much counsel to beware of being gobbled up by long-legged storks, and trod on by impolite men, and struck at by bad boys.

"Even in the Capital there are boors," said Father Frog.

Now it so happened that the old Frog from Kioto and the "lion's cub" from Osaka started each from his home at the same time. Nothing of importance occurred to either of them until, as luck would have it, they met on a hill near Hashimoto, which is half-way between the two cities. Both were footsore, and websore, and very tired, especially about the hips, on account of the unfroglike manner of walking, instead of hopping as they had been used to.

"*Ohio gozarimasu*," said the "lion's cub" to the old Frog, by way of "good-morning," as he fell on all-fours and bowed his head to the ground three times, squinting up over his left eye, to see if the other Frog was paying equal deference in return.

"Yes, good-day," replied the Kioto Frog.

"It is rather fine weather to-day," said the youngster.

"Yes, it is very fine," replied the old fellow.

"I am Gamataro, from Osaka, the oldest son of Lord Bullfrog, Prince of the Lotus-Ditch."

"Your Lordship must be weary with your journey. I am Sir Frog of the Well in Kioto. I started out to see the 'great ocean' from Osaka; but, I declare, my hips are so dreadfully tired that I believe that I'll give up my plan and content myself with a look from this hill."

The truth must be owned that the old Frog was not only on his hind legs, but also on his last legs, when he stood up to look at Osaka; while the youngster was tired enough to believe anything. The old fellow, wiping his face, spoke up:

"Suppose we save ourselves the trouble of the

journey.   I have been told that this hill is half-way between the two cities, and while I see Osaka and the sea, you can get a good look at Kioto."

" Happy thought ! " said the Osaka Frog.

Then both reared themselves upon their hind-legs, once more, and stretching upon their toes, body to body, and neck to neck, propped each other up, rolled their goggles and looked steadily, as they supposed, on the places which they each wished to see.   Now every one knows that a frog has eyes mounted in that part of his head which is *front when he is down and back when he stands up.*

Long and steadily they gazed, until, at last, their toes being tired, they fell down on all-fours.

" I declare ! " said the older Frog, " Osaka looks just like Kioto ; and as for ' the great ocean ' those stupid maids talked about, I don't see any at all, unless they mean that strip of river that looks for all the world like the Yodo. I don't believe there is any ' great ocean ' ! "

" As for my part," said the other, " I am satisfied that it's all folly to go further ; for Kioto is as like Osaka as one grain of rice is like another."

Thereupon both congratulated themselves upon the happy labor-saving expedient by which they had spared themselves a long journey, much leg-weariness, and some danger. They departed, after exchanging many compliments ; and, dropping again into a frog's hop, they leaped back in half the time—the one to his well and the other to his pond. There each told the story of both cities looking exactly alike ; thus demonstrating the folly of those foolish folks called Men. As for the old gentleman in the lotus-pond, he was so glad to get the "cub" back again that he never again tried to reason out the problems of philosophy.

And so to this day the frog in the well knows not and believes not in the "great ocean." Still do the babies of frogs become but frogs. Still is it vain to teach the reptiles philosophy ; for all such labor is "like pouring water in a frog's face."

THE CHILD OF THE THUNDER

IN among the hills of Echizen, within sight of
the snowy mountain called Hakuzan, lived
a farmer named Bimbo. He was very poor,
but frugal and industrious ; and was fond of
children though he had none himself. He
longed to adopt a son to bear his name, and
often talked the matter over with his wife, but
being so dreadfully poor both thought it best not
to adopt any, until they had bettered their condition and increased the area of their land.   For
all the property Bimbo owned was the earth in
a little gully, which he himself was reclaiming.
A tiny rivulet, flowing from a spring in the
crevice of the rocks above, after trickling over
the boulders, rolled down the gully to join a
brook in the larger valley below.   Bimbo had
with great labor, after many years, made dams
or terraces of stone, inside which he had thrown
soil, partly got from the mountain sides, but
mainly carried in baskets on the backs of himself and his wife, from the valley below.   By
such weary toil, continued year in and year out,

small beds of soil were formed, in which rice could be planted and grown. The little rivulet supplied the needful water; for rice, the daily food of laborer and farmer, must be planted and cultivated in soft mud under water. So the little rivulet, which once leaped over the rock and cut its way singing to the valley, now spread itself quietly over each terrace, making more than a dozen descents before it reached the fields below.

Yet after all his toil for a score of years, working every day from the first croak of the raven, until the stars came out, Bimbo and his wife owned less than an acre of terrace land. Sometimes a summer would pass, and little or no rain fall; then the rivulet dried up and crops failed. It seemed all in vain that their backs were bent and their foreheads seamed and wrinkled with care. Many a time did Bimbo have hard work of it even to pay his taxes, which sometimes amounted to half his crop. Many a time did he shake his head, muttering the discouraged farmer's proverb, " A new field gives a scant crop," the words of which mean also, " Human life is but fifty years."

One summer day after a long drought, when

the young rice sprouts were turning yellow at the tips, the clouds began to gather and roll, and soon a smart shower fell, the lightning glittered, and the hills echoed with claps of thunder. But Bimbo, hoe in hand, was so glad to see the rain fall, and the pattering drops felt so cool and refreshing, that he worked on, strengthening the terrace to resist the little flood about to come.

Pretty soon the storm rattled very near him, and he thought he had better seek shelter, lest the thunder should strike and kill him. For Bimbo, like all his neighbors, had often heard stories of the shaggy god of the thunder-drums, who lives in the skies and rides on the storm, and sometimes kills people by throwing out of the clouds at them a terrible creature like a cat, with iron-like claws and a hairy body.

Just as Bimbo threw his hoe over his shoulder and started to move, a terrible blinding flash of lightning dazzled his eyes. It was immediately followed by a deafening crash, and the thunder fell just in front of him. He covered his eyes with his hands, but finding himself unhurt, uttered a prayer of thanks to Buddha for safety. Then he uncovered his eyes and looked down at his feet.

There lay a little boy, rosy and warm.

There lay a little boy, rosy and warm, crowing in the most lively manner, and not frightened by the rain in the least. The farmer's eyes opened very wide, but happy and nearly surprised out of his senses, he picked up the child tenderly in his arms, and took him home to his old wife.

"Here's a gift from Heaven," said Bimbo; "we'll adopt him as our own son and call him Rai-taro," which means "the child of the thunder."

The wife also was delighted with the pretty boy, and never tired of caring for him. So Raitaro lived with them and became a very dutiful and loving child. He was as kind and obedient to his foster-parents as though he had been born in their house. He never liked to play with other children, but kept all day in the fields with his foster-father, sporting with the rivulet and looking at the clouds and sky. Even when the strolling players and the "Lion of Corea" came into the village, and every boy and girl and nurse and woman was sure to be out in great glee, the child of the thunder stayed up in the field, or climbed on the high rocks to watch the sailing of the birds and the flowing of the water and the river far away.

And now great prosperity came to the farmer, and he laid it all to the sweet child who had fallen to him from the clouds. It was very curious that rain often fell on Bimbo's field when none fell elsewhere; so that Bimbo grew rich. He believed that the boy Raitaro beckoned to the clouds, and they shed their rain for him alone.

A good many summers passed by, and Raitaro had grown to be a tall and handsome lad, almost a man and eighteen years old. On his birthday the old farmer and the good wife made a little feast for their foster-child. They ate and drank and talked of the thunder-storm, out of which Raitaro was born.

Finally the young man said solemnly:

" My dear parents, I thank you very much for your kindness to me, but I must now say farewell. I hope you will always be happy."

Then, in a moment, before they had a chance to ask him what he meant, all trace of a human form had disappeared, and floating in the air they saw a tiny white dragon, which hovered for a moment above them and then flew away. The old couple ran out of doors to watch it, and it seemed to their astonished gaze to grow larger as it went away. Bigger and bigger it grew, taking its course to the hills above, where the piled-up white clouds, which form on a summer's afternoon, seemed built up like towers and castles of silver. Toward one of these the dragon moved, until, as they watched his form, now grown to a mighty size, it disappeared from view.

The farmer and his wife knelt in reverence and said farewell, with tears in their eyes, yet with a strange peace in their hearts. After this, as they were now old and white-headed, they ceased from their toil and lived in comfort all the rest of their days. When they died their ashes were laid away in the cemetery of the temple yard, and their tomb was carved in the form of a white dragon, which in spite of mosses and lichens may still be seen among the ancient monuments of the little hamlet.

THE TONGUE-CUT SPARROW

THERE was once an old man who had a wife with a very bad temper. She did not have any children, and would not take the trouble to adopt a son. So for a little pet he kept a tiny sparrow, and fed it with great care. The woman, not satisfied with scolding her husband, hated the sparrow. Her temper was especially bad on wash days, when her back and knees were strained over the low tub, which rested on the ground.

One day while the man was gone to his work in the rice-fields, the wife was washing the clothes, and had made some starch, and set it in a red wooden bowl to cool. While her back was turned, the sparrow hopped down on the edge of the bowl, and pecked at some of the starch. In a rage the woman seized a pair of scissors and cut off the tip of the sparrow's tongue. Flinging the bird in the air she cried out, " Now be off with you ! " So the poor sparrow, all bleeding, flew away.

When the man came back and found the bird
gone, he made a great ado. He asked his wife,
and she told him what she had done and why.
The sorrowful old man grieved sorely for his pet,
and after looking in every place and calling it by
name, gave it up as lost.

Days and weeks and months sped by, and
the man was still older and more wrinkled,
when one day while wandering over the mountains he again met his sparrow. " Good-morning ! " he cried ; and to his surprise and delight
the sparrow answered him. The clipped tongue
had given the bird power of speech. Then each
bowed low and made mutual inquiries as to
health. The sparrow begged the man to visit
his humble abode, and meet his wife and two
daughters.

The man went with him and found a nice
little house with a bamboo garden, tiny waterfall, stepping stone and everything complete.
Then Mrs. Sparrow brought in slices of sugar-
jelly, rock-candy, sweet potato custard, and a
bowl of hot starch sprinkled with sugar, and a
pair of chopsticks on a tray. Miss Sparrow, the
elder daughter, brought the tea-caddy and tea-
pot, and in a snap of the fingers had a good cup

of tea ready, which she offered on a tray, kneel-ing.

"Please help yourself. The refreshments are very poor, but I hope you will excuse our plainness," said Mother Sparrow. The de-lighted old man, wondering in himself at such a polite family of sparrows, ate heartily, and drank several cups of tea. Finally, on being pressed, he remained all night.

For several days he enjoyed a visit at the sparrow's home. He looked at the landscapes and the moonlight, feasted to his heart's con-tent, and played checkers with the little daughter. In the evening Mrs. Sparrow would bring out the refreshments and the wine, and seat the guest on a silken cushion, while she played the guitar. Mr. Sparrow and his two daughters danced, sang, and made merry until the man leaning on the velvet arm-rest forgot his cares, his old limbs and his wife's tongue, and felt like a youth again.

But on the fifth day he said he must go home. His host was sorry to hear this, but brought out two baskets made of plaited rattan, such as are used in traveling, carried on men's shoulders. Placing them before his guest, he said, " Please do me the honor to accept a parting gift. Take either one you prefer."

Now one basket was heavy, and the other light. The old man, not being greedy, said he would take the lighter one. So with many thanks and bows and good-byes, he set off homeward.

He reached his hut safely, but instead of a kind welcome his wife began to scold him for being away so long. He begged her to be quiet, and telling of his visit to the sparrows, opened the basket, while the scowling beldame held her tongue, out of sheer curiosity.

Oh, what a splendid sight ! There were gold and silver coin, and gems, and coral, and crystal, and amber, and a never-failing bag of money, and an invisible coat and hat, and rolls of books, and all manner of precious things. It seemed that they never would reach the bottom of that magic basket.

At the sight of so much wealth, the woman's scowl changed to a smile of greedy joy. " I'll go right off and get another present from the sparrows," said she.

Her husband plead with her not to go, saying that they already had more than enough to last them the rest of their lives. But she would not listen to him. Binding on her straw scandals, and tucking up her skirts, she seized her staff and set off on the road.

Arriving at the sparrow's house, she began to flatter Mr. Sparrow by soft speeches. Of course the polite bird invited her into his house, but nothing but a cup of tea was offered her, while his wife and daughters kept out of sight. Seeing that she was not going to get any good-bye gift, she made bold to ask for one. The sparrow then brought out and set before her two baskets, one heavy and the other light. She eagerly seized the heavier one, without so much as saying "thank you," and carried it back in triumph with her. When she got home she opened it, expecting all kinds of riches.

But the moment she took off the lid, a horrible cuttle-fish rushed at her, a skeleton poked his bony fingers in her face, and a long, hairy serpent, with a big head and lolling tongue, sprang out and coiled around her, cracking her bones, and squeezing out her breath, till she died.

After the good man had buried his wife, he adopted a son to comfort his old age, and with his treasures lived at ease all his days.

THE APE AND THE CRAB

IN the land where neither the monkeys nor the cats have tails, and the persimmons grow to be as large as apples and with seeds bigger than a melon's, there once lived a land Crab in the side of a sand hill. One day an Ape came along having a persimmon seed, which he offered to swap with the Crab for a rice-cake. The Crab agreed, and planting the seed in his garden went out every day to watch it grow. And so fertile is that country, that soon a fine tree had grown up from the seed.

By and by the Ape came to visit the Crab, and seeing the tree laden with the yellow-brown fruit, he begged a few persimmons. The Crab, asking pardon of the Ape, said he could not climb the tree to offer him any, but agreed to give his visitor half, if he would mount the tree and pluck them.

So the Ape ran up the tree, while the Crab waited below, expecting to eat the ripe fruit. But the Ape sitting on a limb first filled his pockets full, and then picking off all the best ones, greedily ate the pulp, and threw the skin and stones in the Crab's face. Every once in a while, he would pull off a green sour persimmon and hit the Crab hard, until his shell was nearly cracked. At last the poor Crab thought he would get the best of the Ape. So when his enemy had eaten his fill until he was bulged out, he cried out,

"Now, Ape, I dare you to come down headforemost. You can't do it."

The other would not take a dare, and at once began to descend, head downward. This was just what the Crab wanted, for all the finest persimmons rolled out of his pockets on the ground. The Crab quickly gathered them up, and with both arms full ran off to his hole. The Ape was very angry at this trick. He kindled a fire, and blew the smoke down the hole, until the Crab was nearly choked and had to crawl out to save his life. Then the wicked Ape beat him soundly, and left him for dead.

The Crab had not been long thus, when three travelers, a Rice-Mortar, an Egg, and a Wasp found him lying on the ground. They carried him into the house, bound up his wounds and while he lay in bed they planned how they might destroy his enemy. They all talked of the matter over their cups of tea, and after the Mortar had smoked several pipes of tobacco, a plan was agreed on.

Taking the Crab along, stiff and sore as he was, they marched to the Ape's castle. The Wasp flew inside, and found that their enemy was away from home. Then all entered and hid themselves. The Egg cuddled up under the ashes in the hearth; the Wasp flew into the closet; the Mortar hid behind the door; the Crab sat beside the fire; and here they waited for the Ape to come home.

Toward evening the Ape arrived, and throwing off his coat (which was just what the Wasp wanted) he lighted a match and kindling a fire hung on the kettle for a cup of tea, and pulled out his pipe for a smoke. Just as he sat down by the hearth to salute the Crab, the Egg in the fire burst and the hot yolk flew all over him and in his eye, nearly blinding him. He rushed out to the bath-room to plunge in the tub of cold water, when the Wasp flew at him and stung his nose. Slipping down, he fell flat on the floor, when the Mortar rolled on him and crushed him to death. Then the victorious party congratulated the Crab on their victory. Grateful for the friendship thus shown, the whole company, Crab, Mortar and Wasp lived in peace together.

The Crab married the daughter of a rich crab that lived over the hill, and a great feast of persimmons was spread before the bride's relatives who came to see the ceremony. By and by a little crab was born which became a great pet with the Mortar and Wasp. With no more apes to plague them, they lived very happily ever afterward.

THE WONDERFUL TEA-KETTLE

A LONG time ago there was an old priest who lived in a temple and was very devout. He was also very poor. He cooked his own rice, boiled his own tea, swept his own floor, and lived frugally as an honest priest should do.

One day the kettle in which he boiled water for his tea got broken, and he did not know what to do, as he had no money to buy a new one. But the next morning, behold! a shiny brass tea-kettle was sitting outside his door. Overjoyed he returned thanks, and built a fire in the square fireplace in the middle of the floor. A rope and chain to hold the rice-pot and tea-kettle hung down from the covered hole in the ceiling which did duty as a chimney. A pair of brass tongs was stuck in the ashes, and soon the fire blazed merrily. At the side of the fireplace, on the floor, was his tray filled with tiny teacups, a pewter tea-caddy, a bamboo tea-stirrer, and a little dipper. The priest having finished sweeping the ashes off the edges of the hearth with a little whisk-broom made of hawk's feathers, was just about to put on the tea when " suzz, suzz," sang the shiny tea-kettle spout; and then " pattari—pattari ! " said the lid, as it flapped up and down, and the kettle swung backward and forward.

" What does this mean ? " said the old priest with a start; for, wonder of wonders, the spout of the kettle had turned into a badger's nose with its big whiskers, while from the other side sprouted out a long bushy tail !

" Ho, ho ! " cried the priest, with a long string of Japanese words which would sound strange to you. And in terror he dropped the tea-caddy, spilling the green tea all over the matting, as four hairy legs appeared under the kettle, and the strange compound, half badger and half kettle, jumped off the fire, and began running around the room. To the priest's horror it leaped on a shelf, puffed out its belly and began to beat a tune with its fore-paws as if it were a drum. The old priest's pupils, hearing the racket, rushed in, and after a lively chase, upsetting piles of books and breaking some of the teacups, secured the badger, and squeezed him into a keg used for storing pickled radishes.

The spout of the kettle had turned into a badger's nose.

They fastened down the lid with a heavy stone, and felt sure that the strong odor of the radishes would kill the beast, for no man could possibly survive such a smell, and it was not likely a badger could.

The next morning the tinker of the village called in and the priest told him about his strange visitor. Wishing to show him the animal, he cautiously lifted the lid of the cask, lest the badger might, after all, be still alive, in spite of the strong vinegar pickles, when lo! there was nothing but the shiny brass tea-kettle. Fearing that the utensil might play the same prank again, the priest was glad to sell it to the tinker, who on his part secretly thought the priest had been dreaming, and was glad to give another kettle in exchange for it, and some cash to boot. He carried it proudly to his junk shop, though he thought it felt unusually heavy.

The tinker went to bed as usual that night with his tiny paper shaded lamp just back of his head. About midnight, hearing a strange noise like the flapping up and down of a pot-lid, he sat up in bed, rubbed his eyes, and there was the bewitched tea-kettle covered with fur and sprouting out legs. In short, it was turning into a hairy beast.

"Don't beat me or shut me in a vinegar keg," it said, "for I am really kind-hearted and wish you well."

"What can I do for you?" asked the tinker.

"Feed me a little rice now and then, and don't put me on the fire as that stupid priest did. Look here."

Going over to a corner of the room and taking a fan from the rack, the badger climbed up on the frame of the lamp, and began to dance on its one hind leg, waving the fan with its fore-paw. It played many other tricks, until the man started up, and then the badger turned into a tea-kettle again.

"I declare," said the tinker as he woke up next morning, and talked the matter over with his wife. "I'll just 'raise a mountain'[1] on this kettle. It certainly is a very highly accomplished tea-kettle. I'll call it by some high-sounding name and exhibit it to the public."

"You've been dreaming," scoffed his wife; "that's only an ordinary brass tea-kettle."

[1] Earn my fortune.

" Just watch it and see," replied the tinker.

So they watched the next night, and sure enough it turned into a badger again.

The delighted tinker hired a professional showman for his business agent, and built a little theatre and stage. Then he gave an order to a friend of his, an artist, to paint scenery, with the sacred mountain Fuji yama in the background and cranes flying through the air, a crimson sun shining through the bamboo, a red moon rising over the waves, with golden clouds and tortoises and such like. Then he stretched a tight rope of rice-straw across the stage, and the handbills being stuck up in all the barber shops in town, and wooden tickets branded with " Accomplished and Lucky Tea-Kettle Performance, Admit One,"—the show was opened. The house was speedily filled, the people coming in parties, bringing their teapots full of tea and picnic boxes full of rice, and eggs, and dumplings made of millet meal, sugared roast-pea cakes, and other refreshments ; because they came to stay all day. Mothers brought their babies with them, for the children enjoyed it most of all.

Then the tinker, dressed up in his wide ceremonial clothes, with a big fan in his hand, came out on the platform, made his politest bow and set the wonderful tea-kettle on the stage. At a wave of his fan, the kettle ran around on four legs, half badger and half kettle, clanking its lid and wagging its tail. How the children shouted; and so should you and I if we could only have been there! Next it turned into a badger, swelled out its body and beat a tune on it like a drum. It danced a jig on the tight rope, and walked the slack rope, holding a fan, or an umbrella in its paw, stood on its head, and finally at a flourish of its master's fan became a cold brass tea-kettle again. The audience were wild with delight, and as the fame of the wonderful tea-kettle spread, many people came from great distances to see it perform.

Year after year the tinker exhibited the wonder until he grew immensely rich. Then he retired from the show business, and out of gratitude took the old kettle to the temple again and deposited it there as a precious relic. The old priest was given a goodly sum of money to do nothing else but take care of it; and all his life it had all the rice and dumplings it wanted.

After his death it turned into an ordinary kettle, and has stayed so ever since. If you don't believe it, you can go to the temple some day and see it for yourself.

BENKEI AND THE BELL

ON one of the hills overlooking the blue sky's mirror of Lake Biwa, stands the ancient monastery of Miidera which was founded over twelve hundred years ago, by the pious Mikado Tenchi.

Near the entrance, on a platform constructed of stoutest timbers, stands a bronze bell five and a half feet high. It has on it none of the writing so commonly found on Japanese bells, and though its surface is covered with scratches it was once as brilliant as a mirror. This wonderful old bell is visited by thousands of people from all parts of Japan who come to wonder at it, for it has a great story to tell.

Over two thousand years ago, say the priests, it hung in a temple in India which Buddha himself built. After his death it got into the possession of the Dragon King, who gave it to the hero, Toda. He however was not able to remove it, so he presented it to the monks at Miidera. With great labor it was brought to the hilltop and hung in this belfry where it rang out every morning and evening, filling the lake and hillsides with sweet melody. Its surface was as smooth and shiny as a looking-glass.

Now it was one of the rules of the Buddhists that no woman should be allowed to ascend the hill or enter the monastery of Miidera. The foolish priests believed that if a woman should enter the door, an evil spirit, also, would slip in at the same time. This was why they made such a severe rule.

But this only made a pretty woman in Kioto want to see it the more. Hearing of the polished face of the bell, this famous beauty resolved to ascend the hill to dress her hair and powder her face in the mirror-like surface. She chose an hour when she knew the priests would be too busy at study of the sacred books to notice her, then she ascended the hill and entered the belfry. Looking into the smooth surface, she saw her own sparkling eyes, her cheeks flushed rosy with exercise, her dimples playing, and then her whole form reflected as in her own silver mirror, before which she daily sat. Charmed as much by the largeness as the brilliancy of the reflection, she stretched forth her hand, and touching her finger-tips to the bell prayed aloud that she might possess just such a mirror of equal size and brightness.

But the bell was outraged at the impiety of the woman's touch, and the cold metal shrank back, leaving a hollow place, and spoiling the even surface of the bell. From that time forth the bell gradually lost its polish, and became dull and finally dark, like other bells.

When big Benkei was a monk, belonging to another monastery, he was possessed of a mighty desire to steal this bell. So one night he went over to Miidera hill, cautiously crept up to the belfry and unhooked the bell from the great iron link which held it. How to get the heavy thing down the mountain was now the question.

Should he let it roll down, the monks at Miidera would hear it bumping over the stones. Nor could he carry it in his arms, for being sixteen feet round, it was too big for him to grasp and hold despite his own huge strength. He could not put his head in it like a candle in a snuffer, for then he would not be able to see his way down.

So climbing into the belfry he pulled out the cross-beam with the iron link, and hanging on the bell put the beam on his shoulder to carry it like a pair of scales.

The next difficulty was to balance it, for he had nothing but his paper lantern to hang on the other end of the beam to balance the bell. It was a prodigiously hard task to carry his burden six or seven miles. It was " trying to balance a bronze bell with a paper lantern," for Benkei's feat has passed into a proverb.

The work made him puff and blow and sweat until he was as hungry as a badger, but he finally succeeded in hooking it up in the belfry at his own monastery.

Then all his fellow priests got up, though at night, to welcome him. They admired his bravery and strength and wished to strike the bell at once to show their joy.

" No, I won't lift a hammer or sound a note till you make me some soup. I am terribly hungry," said Benkei, as he sat down on a cross-piece of the belfry and wiped his forehead with his cowl.

So the priests got out the iron soup-pot, five feet in diameter, and kindling a fire made a huge mess of soup and served it to Benkei. The lusty monk sipped bowl after bowl of the steaming nourishment until the pot was empty.

"Now," said he, "you may sound the bell."

Five or six of the young priests mounted the platform and seized the rope that held a heavy log suspended from the roof. The manner of striking the bell was to pull back the log several feet, then let go the rope, holding the wood after the rebound.

At the first stroke the bell quivered and rolled out a most mournful and solemn sound which as it softened and died away changed into the distinct murmur:

"I want to go back to Miidera! I want to go back to Miidera! I want to go-o ba-a-ck to-o M-i-i-de-ra-ra-a-a-a!"

"Just listen to that!" said the priests. "What a strange bell. It wants to go back. It is not satisfied with our ringing."

"Ah! I know what is the matter," said the aged abbot. "It must be sprinkled with holy water. Then it will be happy with us. Ho! page, bring hither the deep sea-shell full of sacred water!"

So the pure white shell full of the consecrated water was brought, together with the holy man's brush. Dipping it in the water the abbot sprinkled the bell inside and out.

"I dedicate thee, oh, bell, to our service. Now strike," said he, signaling to the bell-pullers.

Again the young men mounted the platform, drew back the log with a lusty pull and let fly.

"Miidera! I want to go back to Miidera!" moaned out the homesick bell.

This so enraged Benkei that he rushed to the rope, waved the monks aside, and seizing the rope strained every muscle to jerk the beam its entire length afield, and then let fly with force enough to crack the bell. For a moment the dense volume of sound filled the ears of all like a storm, but as the vibrations died away, the bell whined out:

"Miidera! I want to go back to M-ii-de-ra!"

Whether struck at morning, noon or night the bell said the same words. No matter when, by whom, how hard or how gently it was struck, the bell moaned the one plaint as if crying, "I want to go back to Miidera!" "I want to go back to Miidera!"

At last Benkei in a rage unhooked the bell, shouldered it beam and all, and set off to take it back. Carrying the bell to the top of the mountain, he set it down, and giving it a kick rolled it down the valley toward Miidera, and left it there. Then the Miidera priests found it and hung it up again. Since that time the bell has completely changed its note, until now it is just like other bells in sound and behavior.

LITTLE SILVER'S DREAM

L ITTLE SILVER was a girl who did not care for strange stories of animals, so much as for those of wonder-creatures in the form of human beings. Even of these, however, she did not like to dream, and when the foolish old nurse would tell her ghost stories at night, she was terribly afraid they would appear to her in her sleep.

To avoid this, the old nurse told her to draw pictures of a tapir on the sheet of white paper which was wrapped around her tiny pillow. These small pillows, you must know, are used by every Japanese girl in order to keep her well-dressed hair from being mussed or rumpled. The nurse told her what many old folks believe,—that if you have a picture of a tapir under the bed, or on the paper pillow-case, you will not have unpleasant dreams, as the tapir is said to eat them. So strongly do some people believe this that they sleep under quilts figured with the device of this long-snouted beast. If in spite of this precaution one should have a bad dream, he must cry out on awaking, "Tapir, come eat, tapir, come eat!" Then the tapir will swallow the dream, and no evil results will happen to the dreamer.

Little Silver listened with open mouth to this account of the tapir, and then making the picture and wrapping it around her pillow, she fell asleep. I suspect that the red rice of which she had eaten so heartily at supper time, until her waist strings tightened, had something to do with her travels in dreamland.

She thought she had gone down to Osaka, and there got on a junk and sailed far away to the southwest, through the Inland Sea. That night the waters seemed full of white ghosts of men and women. Some of them were walking on, and in, the water. Some were running about. Here and there groups appeared to be talking together. Once in a while the junk would run against one of them; and when Little Silver looked to see if he were hurt or knocked over, she could see nothing until the junk passed by, when the ghost would appear standing in the same place, as though the ship had gone through empty air.

Occasionally a ghost would come up to the

side of the ship, and in a squeaky voice ask for
a dipper. While she would be wondering what
a ghost wanted to do with a dipper, a sailor
would quietly open a locker, take out a dipper
having no bottom, and give one every time he
was asked for them. Little Silver noticed a
large bundle of these dippers ready. The
ghosts would then begin to bail up water out of
the sea to empty it in the boat. All night they
followed the junk, holding on with one hand to
the gunwhale, while they vainly dipped up
water with the other, trying to swamp the boat.
If dippers with bottoms in them had been
given them, the sailors said, the boat would
have been sunk. When daylight appeared the
shadowy host of people vanished.

In the morning they passed an island, the
shores of which were high rocks of red coral.
A great earthern jar stood on the beach, and
around it lay long-handled ladles holding a
half-gallon or more, and piles of very large
shallow red-lacquered wine cups, which seemed
as big as the full moon. After the sun had
risen some time, there came down from over the
hills a troop of the most curious looking
people. Many were short, little wizen-faced

folks, who looked very old; or rather, they seemed old before they ought to be. Some were very aged and crooked, with hickory-nut faces, and hair of a reddish gray tint. All the others had long scarlet locks hanging loose over their heads, and streaming down their backs. Their faces were flushed as if by hard drinking, and their pimpled noses resembled huge red barnacles. No sooner did they arrive at the great earthern jar than they ranged themselves round it. The old ones dipped out ladles full, and drank of the wine till they reeled. The younger ones poured the liquor into cups and drank. Even the little infants guzzled quantities of the yellow saké,[1] from the shallow cups.

Then began the dance, and wild and furious it grew. The leather-faced old sots tossed their long reddish-gray locks in the air, and pirouetted round the big saké jar. The younger ones of all ages clapped their hands, knotted their handkerchiefs over their foreheads, waved their dippers or cups or fans, and practiced all kinds of antics, while their scarlet hair streamed in the wind or was blown in their eyes. The dance over, they threw down their cups and

[1] A yellow wine made from rice.

dippers, rested a few minutes and then took another heavy drink all around.

" Now to work ! " shouted an old fellow whose face was redder than his half-bleached hair, and who having only two teeth looked just like an imp. As for his wife, her teeth had long ago fallen out and the skin of her face seemed to have added a pucker for every year since a half century had rolled over her head.

Then Little Silver looked and saw them scatter. Some gathered shells and burned them to make lime. Others carried water and made mortar, which they thickened by a pulp made of paper, and a glue made by boiling fish skin. Some dived under the sea for red coral, which they hauled up by means of straw ropes, in great sprigs as thick as the branches of a tree. They quickly ran up a scaffold, and while some of the scarlet-headed plasterers smeared the walls, others below passed up the tempered mortar on long shell shovels, to the hand mortar-boards. Even at work they had casks and cups of saké at hand, while children played in the empty kegs and licked the gummy sugar left in some of them.

" What is that house for ? " asked Little Silver of the sailors.

" Oh, that is the storehouse in which the King of the Demons lays up all the treasures of life and health and happiness and property, which men throw away or exchange for the saké he gives them. This is what they lose by making funnels of themselves."

" Oh, yes," said Little Silver to herself, as she remembered how her father had said of a certain neighbor who had lately been drinking hard, " He swills saké like a Demon."

She also understood why picnic or " chow-chow " boxes were often decorated with pictures of these imps, with their cups and dippers. For, at these picnics, many men get drunk ; so much so indeed, that after a while the master of the feast orders very poor and cheap wine to be served to the guests. He also replaces the delicate wine cups of eggshell porcelain, with big thick teacups or wooden bowls, for the guests when drunk are liable to shatter the others. Besides they do not know the difference.

She also now understood why it was commonly said of a Mr. Matsu, who had once been very rich but was now a poor sot, "His property has all gone to the Demons."

Just then the ship in which she was sailing struck a rock, and the sudden jerk woke up Little Silver, who cried out, "Tapir, come eat; tapir, come eat!"

No tapir came that she could see, but if he had appeared I fear Little Silver would have been more frightened than she was by her dream of the ghosts; for, the next morning, she laughed to think how they had all their work a-dipping water for nothing. But she never forgot the Demon's treasure-house of lost gold and happiness, whenever she saw any one drinking more saké than was good for him.

THE MAGIC FROG

ONCE upon a time there was a great lord who lived in the Island of the Nine Provinces. He had but one son, a bright little fellow whom the people in admiration nicknamed " Young Thunder." During one of the civil wars, the lord's castle was taken, and he was slain; but by the aid of a servant the boy escaped and fled northward to a neighboring province, where he lived until he grew up to manhood.

For many years the province had been infested with robbers who grew bolder and bolder. One day the faithful servant of Young Thunder was attacked, whereupon he made resistance and was slain by the robbers. The young man now left alone in the world led a wandering life in various parts of the Sunrise Kingdom.

All this time he was consumed with the desire to revive the name of his father, and restore the fortunes of his family. He was exceedingly brave, and an expert swordsman, but his early misfortunes had made him an enemy of the law. So he became chief of a band of robbers, plundered many wealthy merchants, and in a short time was rich in men, arms, and booty. He was accustomed to disguise himself as a beggar, or priest, or traveling tinker, and go in person into the houses of men of wealth, and thus learn all about their gates and guards, where they slept, and in what rooms their treasures were stored, so that success was easy.

Hearing of an old man who lived in the highlands, he started to rob him, and for this purpose put on the disguise of a pilgrim. But before he reached there a great snow-storm forced him to take refuge in a humble house by the way. Entering, he found a beautiful woman, who treated him with great kindness. This, however, did not change the robber's wicked nature. At midnight, when all was still, he unsheathed his sword, and going noiselessly to her room, he found the lady absorbed in reading.

Lifting his sword, he was about to strike at her neck, when, in a flash, her body changed into that of a very old man, who seized the heavy steel blade and broke it in pieces as though it were a stick. Then he tossed the bits of steel away, and thus spoke to the robber who stood amazed but fearless :

" I am a man of magic power, and I have lived in these mountains many hundred years, though my true body is that of a huge frog. I can easily put you to death, but I have another purpose. So I shall pardon you and teach you magic instead. But first you must promise to cease following your evil life."

Then the youth bowed his head to the floor, acknowledged his crimes to the old man, and begged to be received as his pupil. Thus it came about that he dwelt with the magician for several weeks, and learned all the arts of the mountain spirits ; how to cause a storm of wind and rain, and to make a deluge, and to control the elements at will.

He also learned how to govern the frogs, and at his bidding they assumed gigantic size, so that on their backs he could stand up and cross rivers and carry enormous loads.

When the old man had finished instructing him he said, " Henceforth cease from robbing, or in any way injuring the poor. Take from the wicked rich, and those who acquire money dishonestly, but help the needy and the suffer-

He also learned how to govern the frogs.

ing." Thus speaking, the old man turned into a huge frog and hopped away.

What this old mountain spirit bade him do, was just what Young Thunder wished. For you must know, this was in early days before there was much law or order, and people had to protect themselves as best they could. So the young man set out on his journey with a light heart.

" I can now make the storm and the waters obey me, and all the frogs are at my command," he said ; " but alas! the magic of the frog cannot control that of the serpent. I shall have to beware of his poison."

From that time forth the oppressed poor people rejoiced whenever avaricious merchants and extortionate money-lenders lost their treasures. For when a poor farmer, whose crops failed, could not pay his rent or loan, on the date promised, these hard-hearted money-lenders would turn him out of his house, seize his beds, mats, and rice-tub, and even the shrine and images on the god-shelf, to sell them at auction for a trifle, to their minions, who resold them at a high price for the money-lender, who thus got a double benefit. But whenever a miser was robbed, the people said, "The Young Thunder has struck," and then they were glad. In this manner his name soon became the poor people's watchword in those troublous times.

Yet he was always ready to help the innocent and honest, even if they were rich. One day a merchant was sentenced to death, though he was really not guilty. Young Thunder, hearing of it, went to the magistrate and said that he himself was the very man who had committed the robbery. So the man's life was saved, and Young Thunder was hanged on a large oak tree. But during the night, his body changed into a bullfrog which hopped away out of sight, and off into the mountains.

At this time, a young and beautiful maiden lived in the mountain district. Her character was very lovely. She was always obedient to her parents and kind to her friends. Her daily task was to go to the mountains and cut brushwood for fuel. One day while thus busy, singing at the task, she met a very old man, with a long white beard sweeping his breast, who said to her :

"Do not fear me. I have lived in this mountain many hundred years, but my real body is that of a snail.   I will teach you the powers of magic, so that you can walk on the sea, or cross a river however swift and deep, as though it were dry land."

Gladly the maiden took daily lessons of the old man, and soon was able to walk on the waters as if they were the mountain paths.   One day the old man said, " I shall now leave you and resume my former shape.   Use your power to destroy the wicked robbers.   Help those who defend the poor.   I advise you to marry the famous warrior, Young Thunder, and unite your powers with his."

Thus saying, the old man shriveled up into a snail and crawled away.

" I am glad," said the maiden to herself, " for the magic of the snail can overcome that of the serpent.   If Young Thunder, who has the magic of the frog, should marry me, we could then destroy the son of the serpent, the terrible robber, Dragon-coil."

By good fortune, Young Thunder soon met the maiden, and being charmed with her beauty, and knowing her power of magic, he sent a messenger with presents to her parents, asking them to give him their daughter to wife.   The parents agreed, and so the young and loving couple were married.

Hitherto when Young Thunder had wished to cross a river, he had changed himself into a frog and swam across ; or he had summoned a bullfrog before him, which increased in size until it was as large as an elephant.   Then standing erect on its back, he had reached the opposite shore in safety.   Now with his wife's powers the two walked over the waters as though the surface were a hard floor.

Soon after their marriage, war broke out in Japan between two famous clans.   To help them fight their battles, and capture the castles of their enemies, one family besought the aid of Young Thunder, who agreed to serve them and carried their banner.   Their enemies then secured the services of Dragon-coil.

This Dragon-coil was a dangerous and wicked robber whose father was a man, and whose mother was a serpent that lived at the bottom of a lake. He was perfectly skilled in the magic of the serpent, and by spurting venom on his enemies could destroy the strongest warriors.   Collecting thousands of followers, he made great ravages in all parts of Japan, robbing and murdering good and bad, rich and poor alike. Loving war and destruction, he was glad to join forces with one of the warring clans.

Now that the magic of the frog and snail was joined to one army, and the magic of the serpent aided the other, the conflicts were bloody and terrible, and many men were slain on both sides.

On one occasion, after a hard-fought battle, Young Thunder fled and took refuge in a monastery, with a few trusty vassals, to rest a short time. In this retreat a lovely princess was dwelling. She had fled from Dragon-coil, who wished her for his bride. She did not want to marry the son of a serpent, and hoped to escape him. She lived in fear of him continually. Dragon-coil, hearing at one time that both Young Thunder and the princess were at this place, changed himself into a serpent, and distilling a large mouthful of poison, crawled up to the ceiling in the room where Young Thunder lay sleeping, and reaching a spot directly over him poured the venom on his head. The fumes of the poison stupefied him and all his followers. Dragon-coil then changed into a man and seized the princess and made off with her.

Gradually the faithful retainers awoke from their stupor to find their master delirious and near the point of death, and the princess gone.

"What can we do to restore our dear master to life?" This was the question each one asked of the others, as with sorrowful faces and weeping eyes they gazed at his pallid form. They called in the venerable abbot of the monastery to see if he could suggest what might be done.

"Alas!" said the aged priest, "there is no medicine in Japan to cure your lord's disease; but in India there is an elixir which is a sure antidote. If we could get that, the master would recover."

"Alas! alas!" and a chorus of groans showed that all hope had fled, for the mountain in India, where the elixir was made, lay five thousand miles from Japan.

Just then a youth, one of the pages of Young Thunder, arose to speak. He was but fourteen years old, and was a servant out of gratitude, for Young Thunder had rescued his father from many dangers and saved his life. He begged permission to say a word to the abbot, who, seeing the lad's eager face, motioned to him with his fan to speak.

"How long can our lord live?" asked the youth.

"He will be dead in thirty hours," answered the abbot, with a sigh.

"If you will give me leave to go, I will procure the medicine, and if our master is still living when I come back, he will get well."

Now this young page had learned magic and sorcery from the Tengus, or long-nosed elves of the mountains, and could fly high in the air with incredible swiftness. Speaking a few words of incantation, he put on the wings of a Tengu, mounted a white cloud and rode on the east wind to India. He bought the elixir of the mountain spirits, and returned to Japan in one day and a night.

Although Young Thunder was about to expire, at the first touch of the elixir to his face he drew a deep breath, perspiration glistened on his forehead, and in a few moments more he sat up.

Soon he was well, and being now immune to the serpent's poison, he fought a great battle against Dragon-coil and at last killed him. The princess was rescued and restored to her parents. For his brave deeds, Young Thunder was pardoned for all his misdeeds and his father's estate was restored to him. There with his lovely wife he spent his remaining days in quiet and peace. They abjured magic, and instead reared a family of noble sons and daughters. Their name was known with love and honor in all Japan.

HOW THE JELLY-FISH LOST HIS
SHELL

IN the days of old, the Jelly-fish was one of
the retainers in waiting upon the Queen of
the World under the Sea. In those days
he had a shell, and as his head was hard, no
one dared to insult him, or stick him with their
horns, or pinch him with their claws, or scratch
him with their nails, or brush rudely by him
with their fins. In short, this fish instead of
being a lump of jelly, as white and helpless as a
pudding, as we see him now, was a lordly fellow
that could get his back up and keep it high
when he wished to. He waited on the Queen
and right proud was he of his office. He was
on good terms with the King's Dragon, which
often allowed him to play with his scaly tail, but
never hurt him in the least.

One day the Queen fell sick, and every hour
grew worse. The King became anxious, and her
subjects talked about nothing else but her sick-
ness. There was grief all through the water-

world; from the mermaids on their beds of
sponge, and the dragons in the rocky caverns,
down to the tiny gudgeons in the rivers, that
were considered no more than mere bait. The
jolly Cuttle-fish stopped playing his drums and
guitar, folded his six arms and hid away mop-
ing in his hole. His servant the Lobster in vain
lighted his candle at night, and tried to induce
him to come out of his lair. The dolphins and
porpoises wept tears, but the clams, oysters, and
limpets shut up their shells and did not even
wiggle. The flounders and skates lay flat on the
ocean's floor, never even lifting up their noses.
The Squid wept a great deal of ink, and the
Jelly-fish nearly melted to pure water. The
Tortoise was patient and offered to do anything
for the relief of the Queen.

But nothing could be done. The Cuttle-fish
who professed to be " a kind of a " doctor, offered
the use of all his cups to suck out the poison, if
that were the trouble.

But it wasn't. It was internal, and nothing
but medicine that could be swallowed would
reach the disease.

At last some one suggested that the liver of a
Monkey would be a specific for the royal sick-

ness, and it was resolved to try it.   The Tortoise, who was the Queen's messenger, because he could live on both land and water, swim or crawl, was summoned.   He was told to go upon earth to a certain mountain, catch a monkey and bring him alive to the Under-world.

Off started the Tortoise on his journey to the earth, and going to a mountain where the monkeys lived, squatted down at the foot of a tree and pretended to be asleep though keeping his claws and tail out.   There he waited patiently, well knowing that curiosity and the monkey's love of tricks would bring one within reach of his talons.   Pretty soon, a family of chattering monkeys came running along among the branches overhead, when suddenly a young fellow caught sight of the sleeping Tortoise.

" Is it possible ? " said the long-handed fellow, " here's fun !   Let's tickle the old fellow's back and pull his tail."

All agreed, and forthwith a dozen monkeys, joining hand over hand, made a long ladder of themselves until they just reached the Tortoise's back.   They didn't use their tails, for Japanese monkeys have none, except stumps two inches long.   However, he who was to be the tail end of this living rope, when all was ready, crawled along and slipped over the whole line, whispering as he slid :

" 'Sh ! don't chatter or laugh, you'll wake him up."

Now the Monkey expected to hold on the living pendulum by one long hand, and swinging down with the other, to pull the Tortoise's tail, and see how near he could come to his snout without being snapped up. For he well knew that a tortoise could neither jump off its legs nor climb a tree.

One ! Two ! The monkey pendulum swung back and forth without touching.

Three ! Four ! The Monkey's fingernails scratched the Tortoise's back. Yet old Hard Shell pretended to be sound asleep.

Five ! Six ! The Monkey caught hold of the Tortoise's tail and jerked it hard. Old Tortoise now moved out its head a little, as if still only half awake.

Seven ! Eight ! This time the Monkey intended to pull the Tortoise's head, when just as he came within reach, the Tortoise snapped him, held him in his claws, and as the monkey pendulum swung back he lost his hold. In an instant he was jerked loose, and fell head-foremost to the ground, half stunned.

Frightened at the loss of their end link, the other monkeys of the chain wound themselves up like a windlass over the branches, and squatting on the trees, set up a doleful chattering.

" Now," said the Tortoise, " I want you to go with me. If you don't, I'll eat you up. Get on my back and I'll carry you; but I must hold your paw in my mouth so you will not try to run away."

Half frightened to death, the Monkey obeyed, and the Tortoise trotted off to the sea, swam to the spot over the Queen's palace, and in a fillip of the finger was down in the gardens of the Under World.

The Queen hearing of the Monkey's arrival thanked the Tortoise, and commanded her cook and baker to feed him well and treat him kindly, for the Queen felt really sorry because he was to lose his liver.

As for the unsuspecting Monkey he enjoyed himself very much, and ran around everywhere amusing the star-fishes, clams, oysters, and other pulpy creatures that could not run, by his rapid climbing of the rocks and coral bushes, and by rolling over the sponge beds and cutting all manner of antics. They had never before seen anything like it. Poor fellow! he would not have been so frolicsome if he had known what was in store for him.

All this time however the Jelly-fish pitied him in his heart, and could hardly keep what he knew to himself. Seeing the Monkey in one of his gayest moods, the Jelly-fish squeezed up near him and said :

" Excuse my addressing you, but I feel very sorry for you because you are to be put to death."

" Why ? " said the Monkey. " What have I done ? "

" Oh, nothing," said the Jelly-fish, " only our Queen is sick and she wants your liver for medicine."

Then if ever any one saw a sick looking monkey it was this one. As the Japanese still say, " His liver was smashed." He felt dreadfully afraid. He put his hands over his eyes, and immediately began to plan how to save both life and liver !

After a while the clever fellow began to see a

way out. Clapping his hand to his stomach he ran into the hall of the Queen's palace and began to weep bitterly. Just then the Tortoise, passing by, saw his captive.

" What are you crying about ? " he asked.

" Boohoo ! " cried the Monkey. " When I left my home on the earth, I forgot to bring my liver with me, but hung it upon a tree, and now my liver will decay and I'll die. Boohoo-hoo ! " and the poor Monkey's eyes became red as a fish's and streamed with tears.

When the Tortoise told the Queen's courtiers what the Monkey had said, their faces fell.

" Why, here's a pretty piece of business ! The Monkey is of no use without his liver. We must send him after it."

So they dispatched the Tortoise to the earth again, the Monkey sitting a-straddle of his back. They came to the mountain again, and the Tortoise being a little lazy waited at the foot while the Monkey scampered off, saying he would be back in an hour. The two creatures had become so well acquainted that the old Hard Shell fully trusted the lively little fellow.

But instead of an hour the Tortoise waited till evening. No Monkey came. So finding himself fooled, and knowing all the monkeys would take the alarm, he waddled back and told the Queen all about it.

"Then," said the Queen after reprimanding her messenger for his silly confidence, " the Monkey must have got wind of our intention to use his liver, and what is more, some one of my servants must have told him."

So the Queen issued an order commanding all her subjects to appear before the Dragon-King of the World under the Sea. Whoever did this wicked thing, must be punished speedily.

Obedient to this command, the fish and sea animals of all sorts, that swam, crawled, rolled, or moved in any way, appeared before the Dragon-King, and his Queen—all except the Jelly-fish. This convinced the Queen that the Jelly-fish was the guilty one. She ordered the culprit to be brought into her presence, and before all her retainers, she cried out :

" You leaky-tongued wretch, for your crime of betraying the confidence of your sovereign, you shall no longer remain among shell-fish. I condemn you to lose your shell."

Then she stripped off his shell, and left the poor Jelly-fish entirely naked and ashamed.

" Be off, you telltale ! " she ended.   " Hereafter all your children shall be as soft and defenceless as yourself."

The poor Jelly-fish blushed crimson, squeezed himself out, and swam off out of sight.   Since that time all jelly-fishes have had no shells.

LORD CUTTLE-FISH'S CONCERT

DESPITE the loss of the Monkey's liver, the Queen of the World under the Sea, after careful attention and long rest, got well again, and was able to be about her duties and govern her kingdom. The news of her recovery created the wildest joy in the Underworld, and from tears and gloom and silence, the caves echoed with laughter, and the spongebeds with music. Every one had on a " white face." Drums, flutes and banjos, which had been hung up on coral branches, or packed away in shell boxes, were taken down, or brought out, and right merrily were they thrummed. The pretty maids of the Queen put on their ivory thimble-nails, and the Queen again listened to the sweet melodies on the harp, while down among the smaller fry of fishy retainers and the scullions of the kitchen, were heard the constant thump of the shoulder-drum, the bang of the big drum, and the loud cries of the dancers as they struck all sorts of attitudes with hands, feet and head.

No allusion was openly made either to monkeys, tortoises, or jelly-fish. This would not have been polite. But the Jelly-fish, in a distant pool in the garden, could hear a merry mocking song which he felt to be directed against himself.

But none of these musical performances were worthy of the Queen's notice although as evidences of the joy of her subjects they did very well. A great many entertainments were gotten up to amuse the finny people, but the Queen was present at none of them except the one about to be described. How and why she became a spectator shall also be told.

One night the Queen was sitting in the pink drawing-room, arrayed in her queenly robes, for she was almost recovered and expected to walk out in the evening. Everything in the room, except a vase of green and golden colored sponge-plant, and a plume of glass-thread, was of a pink color. Then there was a pretty rockery made of a pyramid of pumice, full of embossed rosettes of living sea-anemones of scarlet, orange, gray, and black colors, which were trained to fold themselves up like an umbrella, or blossom out like crysanthemums, at certain hours of the day, or when touched, behaving just like four o'clocks and sensitive plants.

All the furniture and hangings of the rooms were pink. The floor was made of mats woven from strips of mother-of-pearl, bound at the sides with an inch border of pink coral. The ceiling was made of the rarest of pink shells wrought into flowers and squares. The walls were decorated with the same material, representing sea-scenes, jewels, and tortoise-shell patterns. In the alcove was a bouquet of seaweed of richest dyes, and in the nooks was an open cabinet holding several of the Queen's own treasures, such as a tiara which looked like woven threads of crystal and a toilet box and writing case made of solid pink coral. The gem of all was a screen having eight folds, on which were depicted her palace and throne-room, the visit of Toda, and the procession of the Queen, nobles, and grandees that escorted the brave archer, when he took his farewell to return to earth.

The Queen sat on the glistening sill of the wide window looking out over her gardens, her two maids sitting at her feet. Presently the sound of music wafted through the coral groves and crystal grottoes reached her ear.

"How wonderful this is!" exclaimed the Queen, half aloud. "What strange music is it I hear? It is neither guitar nor drum nor singing. It seems to be a mixture of all. Harken! It sounds as if a band with many instruments were playing, and a chorus were singing."

True enough! It was the most curious music ever heard in the Under-world, for to tell the truth the voices were not in perfect accord, though all kept good time. The sound seemed to issue from the mansion of Lord Cuttle-fish, the palace physician. The Queen's curiosity was roused.

"I shall go and see what it is," said she, as she rose up. Then she recollected, and exclaimed: "O, no, it would not be proper for me to be seen in public at this hour of the evening, and if it is in Lord Cuttle-fish's mansion, I could not enter without a retinue. No, it would be beneath my dignity."

Curiosity, however, got the better of the Queen and off she started with only her two maids who held aloft over her head the long pearl-handled fans made of white shark's fins. She had decided to go incognito.

"Besides," thought she, "perhaps the concert is

outside, in the garden. If so, I can look down
and see from the great green rock that overlooks
it, and my lord the King need not know of it."

The Queen walked over her pebbled garden
walk, avoiding the great high road. The sound
of the drums and voices grew louder as she advanced, until when she reached the top of a
green rock back of Lord Cuttle-fish's garden,
the whole performance was open to her view.

It was so funny, and the Queen was so overcome at the comical sight, that she nearly fell
down in her merriment. She utterly forgot her
dignity, and laughed till the tears ran down her
face. She was so afraid she would scream out,
that she nearly choked herself with her sleeve,
while her alarmed maids, though meaning nothing by their acts but friendly help, slapped her
on the back to give her breath. And this is
what she saw.

There, at the top of a high green rock all
covered with barnacles, on a huge tuft of sponge,
sat Lord Cuttle-fish, playing on three musical
instruments at once. His great speckled head,
six feet high, like a huge bag upside down, was
bent forward to read the notes of his music
book by the light of a wax candle, which was

stuck in the feelers of a prickly Lobster, and patiently held. Of his six pulpy arms one long one ran down like the trunk of an elephant, fingering along the pages of a music book. Two others were used to play the guitar. The small double drum was held by one arm on his shoulder and neck, while still another arm curled up in a bunch, punched it like a fist. Below him was a bass drum, set in a frame, and in his last arm was clutched a heavy drumstick which pounded out a tremendous noise. There the old fellow sat with his head bobbing, and all his six cuppy arms in motion, his rolling blue eyes ogling the notes, and his mouth like an elephant's, screeching out the words of the song.

All this time, in front of Lord Cuttle-fish, sat the Lobster holding up the light, and nodding his head in time to the music.

But the audience, or rather the orchestra, was the funniest part of all. They could not be called listeners, for they were all performers. On the left was the lusty red-faced Bream with its gills wide open, singing at the top, or rather at the bottom, of its throat, and beating time by flapping its wide fins. A little Gudgeon, just behind silent and fanning itself with a blue flat fan, had disgracefully broken down on a high note.   Next on the right was a long-nosed Gar-fish singing alto, and proud of its slender form.   In the foreground squatted a great fat Frog with big bulging eyes, singing bass, and leading the choir by flapping his webbed fingers up and down, with his frightful cavern of a mouth wide open.   Next, sat the stately and dignified Mackerel, rather scandalized at the whole affair, who kept very still, refusing to join in.   At the Mackerel's right fin, squeaked out the stupid flat-headed Globe-fish with her big eye impolitely winking at the servant-maid just bringing in refreshments ; for the truth was, all were very thirsty after so much vocal exercise.

Just behind the Herring, with one eye on Lord Cuttle-fish and one on the coming refreshments, was the Skate.   The truth must be told that the entire right wing of the orchestra was very much demoralized by the smell of the steaming tea and eatables just about to be served. The Tortoise though continuing to sing, impolitely turned its head away from Lord Cuttle-fish, and its back to the Frog that acted as precentor.   The Sucker, though very homely and bloated with fat, kept on in the chorus, and pretended not to notice the waiter and the tray and cups. Indeed, Madame Sucker thought it quite vulgar in the Tortoise to be so eager after the cakes and wine.

Suddenly the music ceased to the relief of all the hungry ones. Lord Cuttle-fish kicked over his drum, unscrewed his guitar, and packed it away in his music box. He then slid along to the refreshment table, and actually amused the company by standing on his head and twirling his six cuppy arms around in the air like a wind-mill.

At this Miss Mackerel was quite shocked, and whispered under her fan to the Gar-fish, " It is quite undignified ! What would the Queen say if she saw it ? " not knowing that the Queen was looking on.

Then all sat down on their tails, propped up-right on one fin, and produced their fans to cool themselves off. The Lobster pulled off the candle stump and ate it up, wiped his feelers, and joined the party.

The liquid refreshments consisted of sweet and clear saké, tea, and cherry-blossom water. The solids were thunder-cakes, egg-cracknels, boiled rice, radishes, maccaroni, lotus-root, and sweet potatoes. Side-dishes were piled up with flies, worms, bugs and all kinds of bait for the small fry—the finny brats that were to eat at the second table. The tea was poured by the servants of Lord Cuttle-fish.

The Queen did not wait to see the end of the feast, but laughing heartily, returned to her palace and went to sleep.

After helping himself with all the cups of his arms out of the tub of boiled rice, until Miss Mackerel made up her mind that he was a glutton, and drinking like a shoal of fishes, Lord Cuttle-fish went home, coiled himself up into a ball, and fell asleep. He had a headache next morning. But the concert and feast had done the Queen more good than all her medicine.

RAIKO AND HIS GUARDS

IN the hill country of Japan grew up a brave young warrior and clever archer who lived more than eight thousand moons ago. On account of his valor and skill in the use of the bow he was called to Kioto, to guard the imperial palace. At that time the Mikado could not sleep at night, because his rest was disturbed by a frightful beast which scared away even the sentinels in armor who stood on guard.

This dreadful beast had the wings of a bird, the body and claws of a tiger, the head of a monkey, a serpent tail, and the crackling scales of a dragon. It came night after night upon the roof of the palace, and howled and scratched so dreadfully that the poor Emperor losing all rest, grew weak and thin. None of the guards dared to face it in hand-to-hand fight, and none had skill enough to hit it with an arrow in the dark, though several of the imperial corps of archers had tried again and again. When the young archer received his appointment, he resolved to fight the dragon come what might. So he strung his bow carefully, sharpened his steel-headed arrows, stored his quiver, and mounted guard alone except for his favorite servant.

It chanced to be a stormy night. The lightning was very vivid, and the thunder-demon was beating all his drums. The wind swirled around frightfully, as though the wind-imp were emptying all his bags. Toward midnight, the falcon eye of the archer saw, during a flash of lightning, the awful beast sitting at the tip of the ridge-pole, on the northeast end of the roof. He bade his servant have a torch of straw and twigs ready to light at a moment's notice, to loosen his sword blade in its sheath, and wet its hilt-pin. Then he fitted the notch of his best arrow into the silk cord of his bow.

Keeping his eyes strained, he soon saw the glare now of one eye, now two eyes, as the beast with swaying head crept along the great roof to the place on the eaves directly over the Mikado's sleeping-room. There it stopped.

This was the archer's opportunity. Aiming about a foot to the right of where he saw the eye glare, he drew his yard-length shaft clear back

This was the archer's opportunity.

to his shoulder, and let fly. A dull thud, a frightful howl, a heavy bump on the ground, and the writhing of some creature among the pebbles, told in a few seconds' time that the shaft had struck flesh. The next instant the servant rushed out with blazing torch and joined battle with his dirk. A short but fierce three-cornered fight ensued, but the warrior's sharp sword soon finished the monster by cutting his throat. Then they flayed it, and the next morning the hide was shown to his majesty.

All congratulated the brave archer on his valor and marksmanship. Many young men, sons of nobles and warriors, begged to become his pupils in archery. The Mikado ordered a noble of very high rank to present him with a famous sword named "The King of Wild Boars," and to give him a lovely maid of honor to wife. He was promoted to be captain of the guard, and given a high-sounding title. But he was also called Raiko, and by this name he is best known to all the boys and girls in Great Japan, who tell many tales of his skill and prowess. Under Captain Raiko were three brave guardsmen, one of whom was named Tsuna. The duty of these men-at-arms was to watch at the gates leading to the palace.

It had come to pass that the Blossom Capital had fallen in a dreadful condition, because the guards at the other gates had been neglected. Thieves were numerous and murders were frequent, so that many good people were afraid to go out into the streets at night. Worse than all else, was the report that hill-demons were prowling around in the dark to seize people by the hair of their heads. Then they would drag them away to the mountains, tear the flesh off their bones, and eat them up.

The worst place in Kioto, to which the two-horned demons came oftenest, was at the south-western gate. To this post of danger, Raiko sent Tsuna, the bravest of his guards.

It was on a dark, rainy, and dismal night, that Tsuna started, well-armed, to stand sentinel at the gate. His trusty helmet was knotted over his chin, and all the pieces of his armor were well laced up. His sandals were girt tight to his feet, and in his belt was thrust the trusty sword, freshly ground, until its edge was like a razor's, and with it the owner could cut asunder a hair floating in the air.

Arriving at the red pillar of the gate, Tsuna paced up and down the stone way with eyes and ears wide open. The wind was blowing frightfully, the storm howled, and the rain fell in such torrents that soon the cords of Tsuna's armor and his dress were soaked through.

The great bronze bell of the temples on the hills boomed out the hours one after another, until a single stroke told Tsuna it was the hour of midnight.

Two hours passed and still Tsuna was wide awake. The storm had lulled, but it was darker than ever. The hour of three rang out, and the soft mellow notes of the temple bell died away like a lullaby wooing one to sleep, spite of will and vow.

The warrior, almost without knowing it, grew sleepy and fell into a doze. He started and woke up. He shook himself, jingled his armor, pinched himself, and even pulled out his little knife from the wooden scabbard of his dirk, and pricked his leg with the point of it to keep awake, but all in vain. Overcome by drowsiness, he leaned against the gate-post, and fell asleep.

This was just what the Demon wanted. All the

time he had been squatting on the cross-piece at the top of the gate waiting his opportunity. He now slid down as softly as a monkey, and with his iron-like claws grabbed Tsuna by the helmet, and began to drag him into the air.

In an instant Tsuna was awake. Seizing the imp's hairy wrist with his left hand, with his right he drew his sword, swept it round his head, and cut off the Demon's arm. Frightened and howling with pain, the creature leaped from the post, and disappeared in the clouds.

Tsuna waited with drawn sword in hand, lest the Demon might come again, but in a few hours morning dawned. The sun rose on the pagodas and gardens and temples of the capitol and the Ninefold Circle of Flowery Hills. Everything was beautiful and bright. Tsuna returned to report to his captain, carrying the Demon's arm in triumph. Raiko examined it, and loudly praised Tsuna for his bravery, and rewarded him with a silken sash.

Now it is said that if a demon's arm be cut off it cannot be made to unite with the body again, if kept apart for a week. So Raiko warned Tsuna to lock it up, and watch it night and day, lest it be stolen from him.

Tsuna went to the stone-cutters who made images of Buddha, mortars for pounding rice, and coffers for burying money, and bought a strong box cut out of the solid stone. It had a heavy lid on it, which slid in a groove and came out only by touching a secret spring. Into this he put the severed arm. Then setting it in his bed-chamber, he guarded it day and night, keeping the gate and all his doors locked. He allowed no one who was a stranger to look at the trophy.

Six days passed by, and Tsuna began to think his prize was sure, for were not all his doors tight shut? So he set the box out in the middle of the room, and twisting some rice-straw fringe in token of sure victory and rejoicing, he sat down in ease before it. He took off his armor and put on his court robes. During the evening, but rather late, there was a feeble knock like that of an old woman at the gate outside.

Tsuna cried out, " Who's there? "

The squeaky voice of his aunt, as it seemed, who was a very old woman, replied, " I want to see my nephew, to praise him for his bravery in cutting the Demon's arm off."

So Tsuna let her in and carefully locking the door behind her, helped the old crone into the room, where she sat down on the mats in front of the box and very close to it.   Then she grew very talkative, and praised her nephew's exploit, until Tsuna felt very proud.

All the time the old woman's left shoulder was covered with her dress while her right hand was out.   Finally she begged earnestly to be allowed to see the limb.   Tsuna at first politely refused, but she urged until he slid back the stone lid just a little.

" This is my arm ! " cried the old hag, turning into a demon, and dragging it out of the casket.

Up she flew to the ceiling, and was out of the smoke-slide through the roof in a twinkling. Tsuna rushed out of the house to shoot her with an arrow, but he saw only a demon far off in the clouds grinning horribly.   While he looked, he saw the severed arm unite again with the body, and the Demon shook *both* fists at him in token of victory.

RAIKO SLAYS THE DEMONS

WHEN the Demon flew away with its arm, Tsuna noticed that it went to the northwest. He told Raiko of the incident, and plans were at once made to seek out and destroy the hill-demons. But just then Raiko fell sick with some strange disease and daily grew weaker and paler. When the Demons found this out they sent a three-eyed Imp to plague him.

This Imp, which had a snout like a hog's, three monstrous blue eyes, and a mouth full of tusks, was glad that the brave soldier could no longer fight the Demons. He would approach the sick man in his chamber, leer horribly at him, loll out his tongue, and pull down the lids of his eyes with his hairy fingers, until the sight sickened Raiko more and more.

But Raiko, well or ill, always slept with his trusty sword under his pillow. He pretended to be greatly afraid, and to cower under the bed-clothes. Then the Imp grew bolder and bolder,

but when it got near his bed, Raiko drew his
blade and cut the enemy across his huge double
nose. This made the Imp howl and run away,
leaving tracks of blood.

When Tsuna and his band heard of their
master's exploit, they came to congratulate
him, and offered to hunt out the Imp and destroy him.

They followed the red drops until they came
to a cavern in the mountains. Entering this
they saw in the gloom a spider six feet
high, with legs as long as a fishing-pole, and as
thick as a giant radish. Two great yellow eyes
glared at them like lamps. They noticed a
great gaping wound as if done by a sword-cut
on his snout.

It was a horrible, nasty hairy thing to fight
with swords, since to get near enough, they
would be in danger of the creature's claws. So
Tsuna went and chopped down a tree as thick
as a man's leg, leaving the roots on, while his
comrades prepared a rope to tie up the monster,
like a fly in a web. Then with a loud yell,
Tsuna rushed at the spider, felled it with a
blow, and held it down with the tree and roots
so it could not bite or use its claws. Seeing

this, Tsuna's comrades rushed in, and bound the monster's legs tight to its body so that it could not move. Drawing their swords they passed them through the spider's body and finished it. Returning in triumph to the city, they found their dear captain recovered from his illness.

Raiko thanked his brave warriors for their exploits, made a feast for them, and gave them many presents. While they were eating he told them that he had received orders from the Mikado to march against the Demons' den, slaughter them all, and rescue the prisoners he should find there. Then he showed them his commission written in large letters,

"I command you, Raiko, to chastise the Demons."

At this time many families in Kioto were grieving over the loss of their children, and even while Tsuna had been away, several lovely damsels had been seized and taken to the Demon's den.

Lest the Demons might hear of their coming, and escape, the four trusty men disguised themselves as wandering priests of the mountains. They covered their helmets with huge hats like washbowls made of straw woven so tightly that no one could see their faces. They covered their armor with very cheap and common clothes, and then after worshiping at the shrines, began their march.

Quite pathless were the desolate mountains, for no one ever went into them except, once in a while, a poor wood-cutter or charcoal-burner; yet Raiko and his men set out with stout hearts. There were no bridges over the streams, and frightful precipices abounded. Once they had to stop and build a bridge by felling a tree, and walking across it over a dangerous chasm. Again they came to a steep rock, to descend which they must make a ladder of creeping vines. At last they reached a dense grove at the top of a cliff, far up to the clouds, which seemed as if it might contain the demon's castle.

Approaching, they found a pretty maiden washing some clothes which had spots of blood on them. They said to her, "Sister, why are you here, and what are you doing?"

"Ah," said she, with a deep sigh, "you must not come here. This is the haunt of Demons. They eat human flesh and they will eat yours. Look there," she continued pointing to a pile of white bones of men, women and children, " you must go down the mountain as quickly as you came." Saying this she burst into tears.

But instead of being frightened or sorrowful, the warriors nearly danced for joy. " We have come here by the Mikado's orders, to destroy the Demons," said Raiko, patting his breast, where inside his dress in the damask bag was the imperial order.

At this the maiden dried her tears and smiled so sweetly that Raiko's heart was touched by her beauty.

" But how came you to live among these cannibal Demons ? " asked Raiko.

She blushed deeply as she replied sadly, " Although they eat men and old women, they keep the young maidens to wait on them."

" It's a great pity," said Raiko, " but we shall now avenge our fellow subjects of the Mikado, as well as your shame and cruel treatment, if you will show us the way up the cliff to the den."

" Willingly," she answered, " if you are not afraid."

They began to climb the hill, but they had not gone far before they met a monster who was a cook in the chief Demon's kitchen. He was carrying a human limb for his master's lunch. Raiko's men gnashed their teeth silently, and clutched their swords under their coats, yet they courteously saluted the cannibal cook and asked for an interview with the chief. The Demon smiled in his sleeve, and beckoned them forward, thinking what a fine dinner his master would make of the four men.

A few feet further, and a turn in the path brought them to the front of the Demon's castle. Among tall and mighty boulders of rock, which loomed up to the clouds, there was an opening in the dense groves, thickly covered with vines and mosses like an arbor. From this point, the view over the plains below commanded a space of hundreds of miles. In the distance the red pagodas, white temple-gables, and castle towers of Kioto were visible.

Inside the cave was a banqueting hall large enough to seat one hundred persons. The floor was neatly covered with new, clean mats of sea-green rice-straw, on which tables, silken cushions, arm-rests, drinking-cups, bottles and many other articles of comfort lay about. The stone walls were richly decorated with curtains and hangings of fine silken stuffs.

At the end of the long hall, on a raised dais, our heroes presently observed, as a curtain was lifted, the chief Demon, of august, yet frightful appearance. He was seated on a heap of luxurious cushions made of blue and crimson crape, stuffed with swan's down. He was leaning on a golden arm-rest. His body was quite red, and he was round and fat like a baby grown up. He had very black hair cut like a small boy's, and on the top of his head, just peeping through the hair were two very short horns. Around him were a score of lovely maidens—the fairest of Kioto—on whose beautiful faces was stamped the misery they dared not fully show, yet could not entirely conceal. Along the wall other Demons sat or lay at full length, each one with his handmaid seated beside him to wait on him and pour out his wine. All of the Demons were of horrible aspect, which only made the beauty of the maidens more conspicuous. Seeing our heroes walk in the hall led by the cook, each banqueter was as happy as a spider, when in his lurking hole he feels the jerk on his web-thread that tells him a fly is caught. Each of them at once poured out a fresh saucer of saké and drank it down.

Raiko and his men separated, and began talking freely with the Demons until the partitions at one corner were slid aside, and a troop of little demons who were waiter-boys entered. They brought in many dishes, and the monsters fell to and ate.   The noise of their jaws sounded like the pounding of rice mills.

Our heroes were nearly sickened at the repast, for it consisted chiefly of human flesh, while the wine cups were made of empty human skulls. However, they laughed and talked and excused themselves from eating, saying they had just lunched.

As the Demons drank more and more they grew lively, laughed till the cave echoed, and sang uproarious songs. Every time they grinned, they showed their terrible tusks, and teeth like fangs.   All of them had horns, though most of these were very short.

The chief Demon became especially hilarious, and drank the health of every one of his four guests in a skull full of wine.   To supply him there was a tub full of saké at hand, and his usual drinking-vessel was a dish which seemed to be as large as a full moon.

Raiko now offered to return the courtesies

shown them by dancing "the Kioto dance," for which he was famous. Stepping out into the centre of the hall, with his fan in one hand, he danced gracefully and with such wonderful ease, that the Demons screamed with delight, and clapped their hands in applause, saying they had never seen anything to equal it. Even the maidens, lost in admiration of the polished courtier, forgot their sorrow, and felt as happy for the time as though they were at home dancing.

The dance finished, Raiko took from his bosom a bottle of saké, and offered it to the chief Demon as a gift, saying it was the best wine of Sakai. The delighted monster drank and gave a sip to each of his lords saying, " This is the best liquor I ever tasted. You must drink the health of our friends in it."

Now Raiko had bought, at the most skilful druggists' in the capital, a powerful sleeping potion, and mixed it with the wine, which made it taste very sweet. In a few minutes all the Demons had dropped off asleep, and their snores sounded like the rolling thunder of the mountains.

Then Raiko rose up and gave the signal to

his comrades. Whispering to the maidens to leave the room quietly, they drew their swords, and with as little noise as possible slew the slumbering Demons one after another. The chief one lying like a lion on his cushions was still sleeping, the snores issuing out of his nose like thunder from a cloud. The four warriors approached him last and like loyal vassals as they were, they first turned their faces toward Kioto, reverenced the Mikado, and prayed for the blessing of the gods who made Japan. Raiko then drew near, and measuring the width of the Demon's neck with his sword found that it would be short. Suddenly, the blade lengthened of itself. Then lifting his weapon, he smote with all his might and cut the neck clean through.

In an instant, the head flew up in the air gnashing its teeth and rolling its yellow eyes, while the horns sprouted out to a horrible length, the jaws opening and shutting like the edges of an earthquake fissure. It flew up and whirled round the room seven times. Then with a rush it flew at Raiko's head, and bit through the straw hat and into the iron helmet inside. But this final effort had exhausted its strength.   Its motions ceased and it fell heavily to the floor.

Anxiously the comrades helped their fallen leader to rise, and examined his head.   But he was unhurt,—not a scratch was on him.   The heroes congratulated each other and after despatching the smaller demons, brought out all the treasure and divided it equally.   Then they set the castle on fire and buried the bones of the victims, setting up a stone to mark the spot. All the maidens and captives were assembled together, and in great state and pomp they returned to Kioto.   The virgins were restored to their parents, and many a desolate home was made joyful, and many a mourning garment taken off.   Raiko was honored by the Mikado in being made a court noble and appointed Chief of the entire garrison of Kioto.   All the people were grateful for his valor.   His three lieutenants were also given posts of honor.   The land was free from evil spirits ever afterward.

THE AMBITIOUS CARP

A FEW years ago there was a boy in Japan, who was very diligent at school and had made fine progress in his studies. He was especially quick at learning Chinese characters, of which every Japanese gentleman who wishes to be called educated must know at least two thousand. For, although the Chinese and Japanese are two very different languages, yet the Japanese, Koreans and Chinese use the same letters to write with, just as English, Italian, French, and Spaniards all employ the same alphabet.

Now the boy's father had promised that when he read through the Ancient History of Japan, he would give him a book of wonderful Chinese stories. The boy performed his task, and his father kept his promise. One day on his return from a journey to Kioto, he presented his son with sixteen volumes, all neatly silk-bound, well illustrated with wood-cuts, and printed clearly on thin, silky mul-

berry paper, from the best wooden blocks.
Japanese books are much lighter and thinner
than ours.

The boy was so delighted with the wonderful
stories of heroes and warriors, travelers and
sailors, that he almost felt himself in China.
He read far into the night, with the lamp inside
of his mosquito curtain; finally he fell asleep,
still undressed, but with his head full of all
sorts of Chinese wonders.

He dreamed he was far away in China, walking along the banks of the great Yellow River.
Everything was very strange.   The people
talked an entirely different language from his
own ; had on different clothes ; and, instead of
the nice shaven head and top-knot of the
Japanese, every one wore a queer long pigtail of
hair, that dangled at his heels.   Even the boats
were of a strange form.   Perched on projecting
rails of the fishing smacks, sat rows of cormo-
rants, each with a ring around his neck.   Every
few minutes one of them would dive under the
water, and after a while come struggling up
with a fish in its mouth, so big that the fishermen had to help the bird into the boat.   The
game was then flung into a basket, and the cormo-

rant was treated to a slice of raw fish, by way of encouragement and to keep the bird from the bad habit of eating the live fish whole. This the ravenous creature would sometimes try to do, even though the ring was put around his neck to prevent it.

It was springtime, and the buds were just bursting into flower. The river was full of fish, especially of carp, ascending to the great rapids or cascades. Here the current ran at a prodigious rate of swiftness, and the waters rippled and boiled and roared with frightful noise. Yet, strange to say, many of the fish were swimming up the stream as if their lives depended on it. They leaped and floundered about, only to be tossed back and left exhausted in the river, where they panted and gasped for breath in the eddies at the side. Some were so bruised against the rocks that, after a few spasms, they floated white and stiff, on the water, dead, and were swept down the stream. Still the shoal leaped and strained every fin, until their scales flashed in the sun like a host of armored warriors in battle. The boy enjoying it as if it were a real conflict of wave and fishes, clapped his hands with delight.

"What is the name of this part of the river?" he asked of an old white-bearded sage standing by and looking on.

"We call it Dragons' Gate," said the sage.

"Will you please write the characters for it," said the boy producing his ink-case and brush-pen, with a roll of soft mulberry paper.

The sage wrote the two Chinese characters, meaning "The Gate of the Dragons," and turned away to watch a carp that seemed almost up into smooth water.

"Oh! I see," said the boy to himself. "There must be some meaning in this fish-climbing."

He went forward a few rods, to where the banks trended upward into high bluffs, crowned by towering firs, through the top branches of which fleecy white clouds sailed slowly along, so near the sky did the tree-tops seem. Down under the cliffs the river ran perfectly smooth, almost like a mirror, and broadened out to the opposite shore. Far back, along the current, he could still see the rapids shelving down. It was crowded at the bottom with leaping fish, whose numbers gradually thinned out toward the centre ; while near the top, close to the edge of

level water, one solitary fish, of powerful fin and
tail, breasted the steep stream.   Now a leap
forward, then a slide backward, sometimes
further to the rear than the next leap made up
for, then steady progress, then a slip, but every
moment nearer, until, clearing foam and ripple
and spray at one bound, it passed the edge and
swam happily in smooth water.

It was inside the Dragons' Gate !

Now came a wonderful thing.   One of the
fleecy white clouds suddenly left the host in the
deep blue above, dipped down from the sky, and
swirling round and round as if it were a water
spout, scratched and frayed the edge of the water
like a fisher's troll.   The carp saw and darted
toward it.   In a moment the fish was trans-
formed into a white Dragon, and, rising into the
cloud, floated off toward heaven.   A streak or
two of red fire, a gleam of terrible eyes, and the
flash of white scales were all that the bewildered
lad saw.   Then he awoke.

" How strange that a poor little carp, a common fish that lives in the river, should become
a great white Dragon, and soar up into the sky,
to live there ! " he mused the next day, as he
told his mother of his dream.

" Yes," said she ; " and what a lesson for you.
See how the carp persevered, leaping over all
difficulties, never giving up till it became a
Dragon.   I hope my son will mount over all ob-
stacles, and rise to honor and to high office
under the Government."

" Oh ! oh ! now I see ! " he cried.   " That is
what my teacher means when he says the
students in Tokio have a proverb :   ' I'm a fish
to-day, but I hope to be a Dragon to-morrow,' and
that's what father means when he says :   ' That
fish's son has become a white Dragon, while I
am yet only a carp.' "

" You are right," replied his mother smiling ;
" and I hope you will be the big carp that becomes a Dragon."

So on the third day of the third month, at the
Feast of Flags, the boy hoisted a great fish, made
of paper, fifteen feet long and hollow like a bag.
It was yellow, with black scales and streaks of
gold, and red gills and mouth, in which two
strong strings were fastened.   It was lifted by a
rope to the top of a high bamboo pole on the
roof of the house.   There the breeze caught it,
and swelled it out round and full of air.   The
wind made the fins work, the tail flap, and the

head tug, until it looked just like a carp trying to swim the rapids of the Yellow River—the symbol of ambition and perseverance to every one who beheld it.

LORD LONG-LEGS' PROCESSION

LOVELY and bright in the month of May, at the time of rice-planting, was the day on which the Baron Long-legs was informed by his chamberlain, Hop-hop, that on the morrow his lordship's retinue would be in readiness to accompany their worshipful Master on his journey to Yedo. This Lord Long-legs was a noble who ruled over four acres of rice-field and whose revenue was ten thousand rice-stalks. His personal retinue, who were all Grasshoppers, like himself, numbered over six thousand, while his court consisted of many nobles, such as Mantis, Beetle, and Pinching-bug. The maids of honor who waited on his Queen Katydid, were Lady-bugs, Butterflies, and Gold-smiths, and his messengers were Fire-flies and Dragon-flies. Once in a while the Beetle was sent on an errand ; but the stupid fellow had a habit of running plump into things, and bumping his head so badly that he always forgot what he was sent for. Besides these, Lord Long-legs had a great many servants in the kitchen

—such as Grubs, Spiders, Toads, and Worms. The entire population of his dominion, including the common folks, numbered several millions, and ranked all the way from Horse-flies down to Ants, Mosquitoes, and Ticks.

Many of his subjects were very industrious and produced fine fabrics, which, however, were seized and made use of by great monsters, called Men. The silver-gray worms kept spinning-wheels in their heads. They had a fashion of eating mulberry leaves, and changing them into fine threads, called silk. The Wasps made paper, and the Bees distilled honey. There was another insect which spread white wax on the trees. These were all retainers or friendly vassals of the Baron in the Castle.

Now it was Lord Long-legs' duty once a year to go up to Yedo to pay his respects to the great Tycoon and to spend several weeks in the Eastern metropolis. I shall not take the time nor tax the patience of my readers in telling about all the bustle and preparation that went on in the mansion of the Baron for a whole week previous to starting. Suffice it to say that clothes were washed and starched, and dried on a board, to keep them from shrinking; trunks and baskets were packed; banners and umbrellas put in order; the lacquered boxes and the brass ornaments dusted off; and swords and spears polished. Every little item was personally examined by the chief inspector. This functionary was a black-and-white-legged Mosquito, who, on account of his long nose, could pry into a thing further than any other of his lordship's officers; and, if anything went wrong, he could make more noise over it than any one else. As for the retainers, down to the very last lackey and coolie, each one tried to outshine the other in cleanliness and smart attire.

The Bumble-bee brushed off the pollen from his legs; and the humbler Honey-bee, after allowing his children to suck his paws, to get the honey sticking to them, spruced up and listened attentively to the orders read to him by the train-leader, Sir Locust, who prided himself on being seventeen years old, and looked on all the others as children. He read from a piece of wasp-nest paper: "No leaving the line to suck flowers, except at halting-time." The Blue-tailed Fly washed his hands and face over and over again. The Lady-bugs wept many tears, because they could not go with the company;

the Crickets chirped rather gloomily, because none with short limbs could go on the journey ; while old Daddy Long-legs almost turned a somersault for joy when told he might carry a bundle in the train. All being in readiness, the procession was to start at six o'clock in the morning. The exact minute was to be announced by the timekeeper of the mansion, Mr. Flea, whose house was on the back of Neko, a great black cat, who lived in the porter's lodge of the castle, near by. Mr. Flea was to notice the opening or slits in the monster's moony-green eyes, which, when closed to a certain width, would indicate six o'clock. Then with a few jumps he was to announce it to a Mosquito friend of his, who would fly with the news to the gatekeeper of the mansion, one Whirligig by name.

So, punctually to the hour, the great double gate swung wide open, and the procession passed out and marched on over the hill. All the servants of Lord Long-legs were out, to see the grand sight. They were down on their knees, saying : "Please go slowly." When their master's palanquin passed, they bowed their heads to the dust, as was proper. The ladies, who were left behind, cried bitterly, and soaked their paper handkerchiefs with tears, especially one fair brown creature, who was next of kin to Lord Long-legs, being an Ant on his mother's side.

The procession was closed by six old Spider daddies marching two by two, who were a little stupid and groggy, having had a late supper, and a jolly feast the night before. When the great gate slammed shut, one of them caught the end of his foot in it, and was lamed for the rest of the journey. He was ordered to walk alongside of old Daddy Long-legs, who hobbled along, with a bundle on his back. These two were the only funny fellows in the procession, and made much talk among bystanders on the road.

This is the order and the way they looked. First there went out, far ahead, a plump, tall Mantis, with a great long baton of grass, which he swung to and fro before him, from right to left, like a drum-major, crying out: " Down on your knees! Get down with you!" Whereat all the Ants, Bugs and Lizards at once bent their forelegs, and the Toads, which were already squatting, bobbed their noses in the dust. Even the Mud-turtles poked their heads out of the water to see what was going on. It was forbidden to any insect to remain on a tall stalk of grass, lest he might look down on His Highness.   So all the Worms and Grubs that lived up in trees or high bushes had to come down to the ground.   Even the Inch-worm had to wind himself up and stop measuring his length, while the line was passing.   And in case of Grubs in the nest or Moths in the cocoon, too young to crawl out, the law compelled their parents to cover them over with a leaf.   It would be an insult to Lord Long-legs to have any one look down on him.

Next followed two lantern-bearers, holding Glow-worms for lanterns in their fore-paws. These were wrapped in cases made of leaves, which they took off at night.   Behind were six Fire-flies, well supplied with self-acting lamps, which they kept hidden somewhere under their wings.   Next marched four abreast the band of little Weevils, carrying the umbrellas of state, which were morning-glories—some open, some shut.   Behind them strutted four green Grass-hoppers, spear-bearers, carrying pink blossoms.

Just before the palanquin were two tall dandies, each of them a Mantis.   High lords themselves and of gigantic stature with arms akimbo and feelers far up in the air, they bore aloft the insignia of their Lord Long-legs.   These fellows

strutted along on their hind legs, their backs as
stiff as hemp stalks, their noses pointing to the
stars, and their legs striding like stilts. The
priest in his robes, a Praying Beetle, who was
chaplain, walked on solemnly.

Meanwhile a great crowd of spectators lined
the path; but all were on their knees. Frogs
and Toads blinked out of the sides of their heads.
The pretty red Lizards glided out, to see the
splendid show; Worms stopped crawling; and
all kinds of Bugs ceased climbing, and came
down from the grass and flower-stalks, to bow
humbly before the train of Lord Long-legs.
Bug mothers hastened, with their bug babies on
their backs, down to the road, and, squatting
down, taught their little ones to put their fore-
paws politely together and bow down on their
front knees. No one dared to speak out loud;
but the Mole-cricket, nudging his fellow under
the wing, said: " Just look at that green Mantis!
He looks as though he would 'rush out with a
battle-ax on his shoulder to meet a chariot.'
See how he ogles his fellow ! "

" Yes; and just behold that bandy-legged
Hopper, will you?   I could walk better than that
myself," said the other.

" 'Sh ! " said the Mole-cricket. " Here comes the lordly palanquin."

Everybody now cast a squint up under their eyebrows, and watched the palanquin go by. It was made of delicately-woven striped grass, bound with bamboo threads, lacquered, and finished with curtains of gauze, made of dragon-fly wings, through which Lord Long-legs could peep. It was borne on the shoulders of four stalwart Hoppers, who, carrying rest-poles of grass, trudged along, with much sweat and fuss and wiping of their foreheads, stopping occasionally to change shoulders. At their side walked a body-guard of eight Hoppers, armed with pistils, and having side-arms of sword-grass. They were also provided with poison-shoots, in case of trouble. Other bearers followed, keeping step and carrying the regalia, consisting of crysanthemum stalks and blossoms. Then followed, in double rank, a long string of Wasps, who were for show and nothing more. Between them, inside, carefully saddled, bridled, and in full housings, was a Horse-fly, led by a Snail, to keep the restive animal from going at a too rapid pace.

Three big, gawky helmet-headed Beetles next

Lord Long-Leg's Procession.

followed, bearing rice-sprouts, with full heads of rice.

" Oh ! oh ! look there ! " cried a little Grub at the side of the road. " See the little Grasshopper riding on his father's back ! "

" 'Sh," said Madam Butterfly, putting one paw on her baby's neck, for fear of being arrested for making a noise.

It was so. The little Hopper, tired of long walking, had climbed on his father's back for a ride, holding on by the feelers and seeing everything.

Finally, toward the end of the procession, was a great crowd of common Hoppers, Beetles, and Bugs of all sorts, carrying the presents to be given in Yedo, and the clothing, food, and utensils for the use of Lord Long-legs on the journey ; for the hotels were sometimes very poor on the high road, and the Baron liked his comforts. Besides, it was necessary for Lord Long-legs to travel with proper dignity. His messengers always went before and engaged lodging-places, as the Fleas, Spiders and Mosquitoes from other localities, that traveled up and down the great high road, sometimes occupied the places first. The procession wound up with the rear-guard of Daddy Long-legs, and the limping Spider. These prevented any insult or disrespect from the rabble. After the line had passed, insects could cross the road, traffic and travel were resumed, and the road was cleared, while the procession faded from view in the distance.

"Mother, what did the worshipful Lord Long-legs look like? I couldn't see him," said little Grub.

"I don't know," replied Madam Butterfly; "I never saw him either, and I don't think anybody else did."

And it was true. All they could see was the palanquin. But it was a fine procession just the same.

THE POWER OF LOVE

QUIET and shady was the spot in the midst of one of the loveliest valley landscapes in the empire, near the banks of the Hidaka River, where stood a famous tea-house. It was surrounded on all sides by glorious mountains, ever robed with deep forest, silver-threaded with flashing water-falls, to which the lovers of nature paid many a visit. Here poets were inspired to write stanzas in praise of the white foam and the twinkling streamlets. Here the priests loved to muse and meditate. Anon merry picnic parties spread their mats, looped their canvas screens, and feasted out of nests of lacquered boxes, drinking the amber saké from cups no larger nor thicker than an egg-shell, while the sound of guitar and drum kept time to dance and song.

The garden of the tea-house was as lovely a piece of art as the florist's cunning could produce. Those who emerged from the deep woods of the lofty hill called the Dragon's Claw, could see in the garden a living copy of the landscape before them. There were mimic mountains, ten feet high, and miniature hills veined by a tiny path, with dwarfed pine groves, clumps of bamboo, a patch of grass for meadow, and a valley just like the great gully of the mountains, times smaller, yet only twenty feet long. So perfect was the imitation that even the miniature irrigated rice-fields, each no larger than a checker-board, were in full sprout. To make this little gem of nature in art complete, there fell from over a rock at one end a lovely little waterfall two feet high, which after an angry splash over the stones, rolled on over an absurdly small beach, all white-sanded and pebbled, threading its silver way beyond, until lost in fringes of lilies and aquatic plants. In one broad space imitating a lake, was a lotus pond, lined with iris, in which the fins of gold fish and silver carp flashed in the sunbeams. Here and there the nose of a tortoise protruded, while on a rugged rock sat an old grandfather surveying the scene with one or two of his grandchildren asleep on his shell and sunning themselves.

The fame of the tea-house, its excellent fare, and special delicacy of its mountain trout, sugar-jelly and well-flavored rice-cakes, drew hundreds of visitors, especially lovers of grand scenery.

Just across the river, which was visible from the veranda of the tea-house, rose the lofty firs that surrounded a Buddhist temple. Hard by was the red pagoda, which peeped between the trees. A long row of paper-windowed and tile-roofed dwellings to the right made up the monastery, in which a snowy eye-browed but rosy-faced old abbot and some twenty priests dwelt, all shaven-faced and shaven-pated, in crape robes and straw sandals, their only food being water and vegetables.

Not the least noticeable of the array of stone lanterns, and bronze images with aureoles round their heads, and incense-burners and holy water tanks, and dragon spouts, was the belfry, which stood on a stone platform. Under its roof hung the massive bronze bell ten feet high. When struck with a suspended log, like a trip-hammer, it boomed solemnly over the valley and flooded three leagues of space with the melody which died away as sweetly as an infant falling in slumber. This mighty bell was six inches thick and weighed several tons.

Of the tea-house across the river, its sweetest charm, and fairest flower was Kiyo, the host's daughter. She was a lovely maiden of but eighteen, as graceful as the bamboo reed swaying in the breeze on a moonlit summer's eve, and as pretty as the blossoms of the cherry-tree. Far and wide floated the fame of Kiyo like the fragrance of white lilies, when the wind sweeping down the mountain heights, comes perfume-laden to the traveler.

As she busied herself about the garden, or as her white socks slipped over the mat-laid floor, she was the picture of grace itself. When at twilight, with her own hands she lighted the gay lanterns that hung in festoons along the eaves of the tea-house above the veranda, her bright eyes sparkling, her red silk under dress half visible through her semi-transparent crape robe, she made many a young man's heart glow with a strange new feeling, or burn with pangs of jealousy. And many came to the tea-house who were not thinking of the tea or scenery.

It was the rule of the monastery that none of the priests should drink saké, eat fish or meat, or even stop at the tea-houses. One young priest had rigidly kept these rules. Fish had never

passed his mouth; and as for saké, he did not
know even its taste. He was very studious and
diligent. Every day he learned ten new Chinese
characters. He had already read several of the
sacred books, had made a good beginning in
Sanskrit, knew the name of every one of the
three thousand three hundred and thirty-three
images in Kioto's most famous temples, had
twice visited the sacred shrines of the Capital,
and had uttered the prayer, "Glory be to the
sacred lotus of the law," counting it on his
rosary, five hundred thousand times. For
sanctity and learning he had no peer among the
young neophytes of the monastery.

Alas for his piety! One day, after returning
from a visit to a famous shrine, as he was passing the tea-house, he caught sight of Kiyo, and
from that moment his pain of heart began. He
returned to his bed of mats, but not to sleep.
For days he tried to stifle his passion, but his
heart only smouldered away like an incense-stick.

Before many days he made a pretext for
passing that way again and again. Hopelessly
in love, he stopped and entered the tea-house.

His call for refreshments was answered by
Kiyo herself!

As fire kindles fire, so priest and maiden were now consumed in one flame of love. To shorten a long story, he visited the inn oftener and oftener, even stealing out at night to cross the river and spend the silent hours with his love.

So passed several months, until a change began to come over the young priest. His conscience began to trouble him for breaking his vows. In the terrible conflict between principle and passion, his soul was tossed to and fro like the feathered seed-ball of a shuttlecock. But conscience was the stronger, and won the victory. He resolved to drown his love and break off his connection with the girl. To do it suddenly, would bring grief to her and a scandal both on her family and the monastery. He must do it gradually to succeed at all.

Ah ! how quickly does the sensitive love-plant know the finger-tip touch of cooling passion ! Kiyo marked the ebbing tide of her lover's regard, and in her first grief and anger a terrible resolve of evil took possession of her soul. She determined to win over her lover by her importunities, and failing in this, to destroy him by sorcery.

One night she sat up until two o'clock in the morning, and then, arrayed only in a white robe, she went out to a secluded part of the mountain where in a lonely shrine stood a hideous scowling image of Fudo, who holds the sword of vengeance and sits clothed in fire. There she called upon the god to change her lover's heart or else show her how to destroy him.

Thence, with her head shaking and eyes glittering with anger like the orbs of a serpent, she hastened to the shrine of Kampira, whose servants are the long-nosed sprites, who have the power of magic and of teaching sorcery. Standing in front of the portal she saw it hung with votive tablets, locks of hair, teeth, various tokens of vows, pledges, and marks of sacrifice, which the devotees of the god had hung up. In the cold night air she asked for the power of sorcery, that she might be able at will to transform herself into the terrible dragon-serpent whose engine coils are able to crack bones, crush rocks, melt iron, or root up trees, and which are long enough to wind round a mountain.

It would be too long to tell how this once pure and happy maiden, now turned to an avenging demon, went out nightly on the lonely mountains to practice the arts of sorcery. The mountain-sprites were her teachers, and she learned so diligently that the chief goblin at last told her she would be able, without fail, to transform herself when she wished.

The dreadful moment was soon to come. The visits of the once lover-priest gradually became fewer and fewer. They were no longer tender hours of love, but were on his part only formal interviews, while Kiyo became more importunate than ever. Tears and pleadings were alike useless, and finally one night as he was taking leave, the priest told the maid that he had paid his last visit.

Immediately the baleful fire of a serpent came into Kiyo's eyes, and the priest turned and fled across the river. He had seen the terrible gleam in the maiden's eyes, and now terribly frightened, hid himself under the great temple bell.

Forthwith Kiyo seeing the awful moment had come, pronounced the spell of incantation taught her by the mountain spirit, and raised her T-shaped wand. In a moment her fair head and lovely face, body, limbs, and feet lengthened out, disappeared, or became demon-like, and a fire-darting, hissing-tongued serpent, with eyes like moons trailed over the ground toward the temple, swam the river, and scenting out the track of the fugitive, entered the belfry, cracking the supporting columns made of whole tree-trunks into a mass of ruins, while the bell fell to the earth with the cowering victim inside.

Then she began winding the terrible coils round and round the metal, as with her wand of sorcery in her hands, she mounted the bell. The glistening scales, hard as iron, struck off sparks as the pressure increased. Tighter and tighter they were drawn, till the heat of the friction consumed the timbers and made the metal glow hot like fire.

Vain was the prayer of priest, or spell of rosary, as all the other bonzes piteously besought great Buddha to destroy the demon. Hotter and hotter grew the mass, until the ponderous metal ran down into a hissing pool of molten bronze; and soon, man within and serpent without, timber and tiles and ropes were nought but a few handfuls of white ashes.

THE TIDE-JEWELS

THE Empress of Japan, wife of the fourteenth Mikado was named Jingu, or Godlike Exploit. She was a wise and discreet lady and assisted her husband to govern his dominions. When the Mikado marched his army against the rebels, the Empress went with him and lived in the camp. One night, as she lay asleep in her tent, she dreamed that a heavenly being appeared to her and told her of a wonderful land in the West, full of gold, silver, jewels, silks, and precious stones. The heavenly messenger told her if she would invade this country she would succeed, and all its spoil would be hers, for herself and Japan.

"Conquer Corea!" said the radiant being, as she floated away on a purple cloud.

In the morning the Empress told her husband of her dream, and advised him to set out to invade the rich land. But he paid no attention to her. When she insisted, in order to satisfy her, he climbed up a high mountain, and looking far away toward the setting sun, saw no land thither, not even mountain peaks. So, believing that there was no country in that direction he descended, and refused to set out on the expedition. Shortly after, in a battle with the rebels the Mikado was shot dead with an arrow.

The generals and captains of the host then declared their loyalty to the Empress as the sole ruler of Japan. She, now having the power, resolved to carry out her darling plan of invading Corea. She called upon all the spirits of the mountains, rivers, and plains to give her their advice and help. Then the fairy of the mountains obeyed and gave her timber and iron for her ships; the fairy of the fields presented rice and grain for provisions; the fairy of the grasses gave her hemp for cordage. The wind-god promised to open his bag and let out his breezes to fill her sails toward Corea. All appeared except Isora, the spirit of the seashore. Again she called for him and sat up waiting all night with torches burning, invoking him to appear.

Now, Isora was a lazy fellow, always slovenly and ill-dressed, and when at last he did come, instead of appearing in state in splendid robes, he rose right out of the sea-bottom, covered with mud and slime, with shells sticking all over him and seaweed clinging to his hair. He gruffly asked what the Empress wanted.

" Go down to the Under-World and beg his majesty, the Dragon King, to give me the two Tide-jewels," she replied.

Now, among the treasures in the palace of the Dragon King of the World under the Sea were two Jewels having wondrous power over the ebbing and the flowing tides. They were about as large as apples, but shaped like apricots, with three rings cut near the top. They seemed to be of crystal, and glistened and shot out dazzling rays like fire. Indeed, they appeared to seethe and glow like the eye of a dragon, or the white-hot steel of the sword-forger. One was called the Jewel of the Flood-Tide, and the other the Jewel of the Ebb-Tide. Whoever owned them had the power to make the tides instantly rise or fall at his word, to make the dry land appear, or the sea overwhelm it, in the fillip of a finger.

Isora dived with a dreadful splash, down, down to the Under-world, and straightway presented himself before the Dragon King. In

The dragon-fishes, taking the ship's cables in their mouths, towed them forward.

the name of the Empress, he begged for the two tide-jewels. The Dragon King granted his request. Producing the flaming globes from his casket, he placed them on a huge shell and handed them to Isora, who brought the Jewels to Jingu. She at once placed them in her girdle.

The Empress now prepared her fleet for the Corean invasion. Three thousand barges were built and launched. This mighty fleet sailed for Corea in the tenth month. The hills of Japan soon began to sink below the horizon, but no sooner were they out of sight of land than a great storm arose. The ships tossed about, and began to butt each other like bulls, and it seemed as though the fleet would be driven back; when lo! the Dragon King sent shoals of huge sea-monsters and immense fishes that bore up the ships and pushed their sterns forward with their great snouts. The dragon-fishes, taking the ship's cables in their mouths towed them forward, until the storm ceased and the ocean was calm. Then they plunged downward into the sea and disappeared.

The mountains of Corea now rose into view. But the army was not to be suffered to land unmolested. Corean spies had informed their king, so that he had made ready. Along the shore were gathered the entire Corean army. Their triangular fringed banners, inscribed with dragons, flapped in the breeze. As soon as their sentinels caught sight of the Japanese fleet, the signal was given, and the Corean line of war galleys moved gaily out to attack the Japanese.

The Empress posted her archers in the bows of her ships and waited for the enemy to approach. When they were within a few hundred sword-lengths, she took from her girdle the Jewel of the Ebbing Tide and cast the flashing gem into the sea. It blazed in the air for a moment, but no sooner did it touch the water, than instantly the ocean receded from under the Corean vessels, and left them stranded on dry land. The Coreans, thinking it was a tidal wave, and that the Japanese ships were likewise helpless in the undertow, leaped out of their galleys and rushed over the sand, and on to the attack. With shouting and drawn swords their aspect was terrible. When within range of the arrows, the Japanese bowmen opened volleys of double-headed, or triple-pronged arrows on the Coreans, and killed hundreds.

But on they rushed, until near the Japanese

ships, when the Empress taking out the Flood-Tide Jewel, cast it in the sea. In the snap of a finger, the ocean rolled up into a wave many tens of feet high and engulfed the Corean army, drowning them almost to a man. Only a few were left out of the ten thousand. The warriors in their iron armor sank like lead in the boiling waves. The Japanese army landed safely, and easily conquered the country. The king of Corea surrendered and gave his bales of silk, jewels, mirrors, books, pictures, robes, tiger skins, and treasures of gold and silver to the Empress. The booty was loaded on eighty ships, and the Japanese army returned in triumph to their native country.

But the Tide-Jewels had, of course, sunk into the sea when the Empress threw them there. Isora seized them at once and returned them to his master.

Soon after her arrival at home, a son was born to the Empress Jingu, whom she named Ojin. He was one of the fairest children ever born of an imperial mother, and was very wise and wonderful even when an infant. As he grew up, he was full of the Spirit of Unconquerable Japan.

The Prime Minister was a very venerable old

man, who was said to be three hundred and sixty years old. He had been the counselor of five Mikados. He was very tall, and as straight as an arrow, when other old men were bent like a bow. He served as a general in war and a civil officer in peace. For this reason he always kept on a suit of armor under his long satin and damask court robes. He wore the bear-skin shoes and the tiger-skin scabbard which were the general's badge of rank, and also the high cap and long fringed strap hanging from the belt, which marked the court noble. He had moustaches, and a long beard fell over his breast like a foaming waterfall, as white as the snows on the branches of the pine trees of Ibuki Mountain.

The Empress wished the little Ojin to live long, be wise and powerful, become a mighty warrior, be invulnerable in battle, and to have control over the tides and the ocean as his mother once had. To do this it was necessary to get back the Tide-Jewels.

So the Prime Minister took Ojin on his shoulders, mounted the imperial war-barge, whose sails were of gold-embroidered silk, and bade his rowers put out to sea. Then standing upright on the deck, he called on the Dragon King to come up out of the deep and give back the Jewels.

At first there was no sign from the waves. The green sea lay glassy in the sunlight, and the water laughed and curled above the sides of the boat. Still the Prime Minister listened intently and waited reverently. He was not long in suspense. Looking down far under the sparkling waves, he saw the head and fiery eyes of a dragon mounting upward. Instinctively he clutched his robe with his right hand, and held Ojin tightly on his shoulder, for this time it was not Isora, but the terrible Dragon King himself who was coming.

What a great honor! The sea-king's servant, Isora, had appeared to the Empress Jingu, but the Dragon King deigned to come in person to her son!

The waters opened; the waves rolled up, curled, rolled into wreaths and hooks and drops of foam, which flecked the dark green curves with silvery bells. First appeared a living dragon with fire-darting eyes, long flickering moustaches, glittering scales of green all ruffled, with terrible spines erect, and out of the joints of the fore-paws were curling jets of red fire. This living creature was the helmet of the Sea King. Next appeared the face of awful majesty and stern mien, as if with reluctant condescension, and then the jewel robes of the monarch. Then rose into view a huge shell, in which, on a bed of rare gems from the deep sea floor, glistened, blazed and flashed the two Jewels of the Tides.

The Dragon King spoke, saying: "Quick, take this casket. I deign not to remain long in this upper world of mortals. With these I endow the imperial prince of the Heavenly line of the Mikados of the Divine Country. He shall he invulnerable in battle. He shall have long life. To him I give power over sea and land. Of this, my promise, let these Tide-Jewels be the token."

Hardly were the words uttered when the Dragon King disappeared with a tremendous splash. The Prime Minister standing erect but breathless amid the crowd of rowers who, crouching at the boat's bottom had not dared so much as to lift up their noses, waited a moment, and then gave the command to turn the prow to the shore.

It came about just as the sea-king had said. Ojin grew up and became a great warrior, invincible in battle and powerful in peace. He lived to be one hundred and eleven years old, and was one of the most famous princes who ever sat upon the throne beneath the sunlit banner of Japan.

THE GRATEFUL CRANE

"FIGHTING sparrows fear not man," as the old proverb says. Yet it was not a sparrow but a crane that fell down out of the air. Near the feet of Musai, the farmer's boy, it lay, as he waded in the ooze of his rice-field, working from daybreak to sundown.

The farmer's boy was used to cranes, for in the plough's furrow on the dry land these long-legged birds walked close behind, not the least afraid in the Mikado's dominions. For who would hurt the white-breasted creature, that every one called the Honorable Lord Crane? The graceful birds seemed to love to be near man, when he worked in the wet or paddy-fields, where under four inches of water the seeds were planted and the rice plants grew. So graceful in all its movements is the crane, that many a dainty little maid, who acts politely, hears herself spoken of as the "bird that rises from the water without muddying the stream."

Musai hurried to the grassy bank at the edge of the paddy-field as fast as he could wade through the liquid mud, to see what was the matter with the crane. Throwing down his hoe, and looking in the grass, he saw that an arrow was sticking in the crane's back, and that red drops of blood dappled its white plumage. Instead of seeming frightened when the man came near, the bird bent down its neck, as if to submit to whatever the farmer's boy should do.

Gently Musai plucked out the arrow and helped the bird to rise, pushing back the undergrowth so that its broad white pinions could have free play. After a few feeble attempts to fly, it spread its wings, rose up from the earth, and after circling several times round its benefactor as though to thank him, it flew off to the mountain.

Musai went back to his work, hoping that in season his labor would yield a good crop. He had his widowed mother to support and must needs toil every day. His one delight was to come home, weary after the long hours of labor in the muddy rice-field, and have a hot bath. This his mother always had ready for him. Then, clean and with a fresh kimono, and a little rest before supper-time, he was ready for a quiet evening with the neighbors.

So in routine the days passed by until autumn was near at hand. One day, returning before the sun was fully set, he found seated beside his mother a lovely girl. In spite of his contemptible appearance after a day's toil, working barelegged in the mire, she welcomed him with the grace of a princess.

Not thinking of returning the salute, in his unwashed condition, he took off his head-kerchief, drew in his breath, and bowing to his mother asked,

" Who is the honorable That Side, and how comes she into this miserable hut ? "

" My son," replied his mother, " though you are a man, you have as yet no wife. Your virtues of obedience, filial reverence, fidelity, and politeness have made you well known. Hence this fair damsel is not unwilling to become your wife. But, without your consent, I could not answer her proposal. What do you think about it ? "

The young farmer, though highly complimented, at first said little, but he thought hard. " Daintily reared, and perhaps of noble birth is she, but should I gratify her desire, how can she bear the poverty to which we are accustomed? Will she be patient, when she has to suffer hunger? Or, shall we be separated, and that which promises love and happiness last only a little while, to pass away, leaving gloom and sorrow behind?"

But as the days slipped along, and when he saw how kind she was to her new mother, ever patient and self-denying in loving reverence, all his fears were driven away like clouds before the wind. So the young man and woman were married.

But when the full autumn time came for the rice ears to fill and round out, nothing was found but husk and shell. The crop was a total failure. With heavy taxes unpaid and no food in the house, starvation loomed before them. By winter, all were in dire distress.

Then the patient wife revealed new powers and cheered her husband, saying,

"I can spin such cloth as was never made in this province, if you will build me a separate room. I cannot weave here, or make the fine pattern of red and white except when alone and in perfect silence. Build me a room, and the money you need will flow in."

The old mother was doubtful as to her

daughter-in-law's project and even Musai was but half-hearted. Yet he went to work diligently. With beam, and wattle, and thatch, floor of mats and window of latticed paper, with walls made tight because well daubed with clay, he built the room apart. There alone, day by day, secluded from all, the sweet wife toiled unseen. The mother and husband patiently waited, until after a week, the little woman rejoined the little family circle. In her hands she bore a roll of woven stuff, white and sheeny, as lustrous and pure as fresh fallen snow. Yet here and there, a crimson thread in the stuff did but intensify the purity of the otherwise unflecked whiteness. Pure red and pure white were the only colors of this wonderful fabric.

"What shall we call it?" inquired the amazed husband.

"It has no name, for there is none other in the world like it," said the fair weaver.

"But I must have a name. I shall take it to the Daimio. He will not buy, if he does not know how it is called."

"Then," said the wife, "tell him its name is 'White Crane's-down cloth.'"

Quickly passed the snowy fabric into the

hands of the lord of the castle, who sent it as a present to the Empress in Kioto. All were amazed by it, and the Empress commanded the donor to be richly rewarded. The farmer husband, bearing a thousand pieces of coin in his bag, hastened home to spread the shining silver at his mother's feet and to thank the wife who had brought him fortune. A feast followed, and for many weeks the family lived easily on the money thus gained. Then, when again on the edge of need, Musai asked his wife if she were willing to weave another web of the wonderful Crane's-down cloth.

Cheerfully she agreed, cautioning him to leave her in privacy, and not to look upon her until she came forth with the cloth.

But alas for the spirit of prying impertinence and wicked curiosity! Not satisfied with having been delivered from starvation by a wife that served him like a slave, Musai stealthily crept up to the paper partition, touched his tongue to the latticed pane, and poked his finger noiselessly through, thus making a round hole to which he glued his eye and looked in.

What a sight! There was no woman at work, but a noble white crane—the same that he had seen in the field, and from whose back he had extracted the hunter's arrow. Bending over the spinning wheel, the bird pulled from her own breast the silky down, and by twining and twisting made it into the finest thread which mortals ever beheld. From time to time, she pressed from her heart's blood red drops with which to dye some strands, and thus the weaving went on. The web of the cloth was nearly finished.

Musai astounded looked on without moving, until suddenly called by his mother, he cried out in response, " Yes, I'm coming."

The startled crane turned and saw the eye in the wall. Throwing down thread and web she moved angrily to the door, gave a shrill scream and flew out under the sky. Like a white speck against the blue hills, she appeared for a little while and then was lost to sight.

Son and mother once more faced poverty and loneliness, and Musai again splashed barelegged in the rice-field.

THE IDOL AND THE WHALE

FROM heels to toes, man's two feet are of the same length and so for all the animal creation. One would think that in measuring metal and for taking the length of cloth, the feet on the yard stick would be alike; but no! in Japan they are not. When you go out shopping and buy cloth or soft goods, you will find the " whale measure " used. Do you go to the lumber or stone yard, or see anything hard measured, then the man pulls out his " metal foot " and marks off the length. There are two inches of difference, but why?

We must go to Kamakura to find out.

The old Buddha image that has stood out in the rain for seven hundred years could tell you, were it to open its metal lips. It is about the tallest piece of bronze in the world, with eyes of pure gold, and a great silver boss on its forehead, that looks like the full moon, and it has eight hundred big curls on its head. These are the snails that kindly coiled themselves on Buddha's head when by thinking too much, in the hot sun of India, he might have been sunstruck.

When the great general, Yoritomo, gave peace to Japan after long wars, he laid out the city of Kamakura. To attract pilgrims to the new capital, he ordered the greatest image of Buddha in all Japan to be reared in his capital. When finished, the sitting figure rose fifty feet in the air. It was ninety-seven feet in circumference, the length of its face was eight feet, and the width from ear to ear seventeen feet, and from knee to knee it measured twelve yards. As for the thumbs, they were three feet round. Over it was built a lordly temple and the columns of camphor wood were covered with gold.

Such a colossal image quickly became the talk of people throughout the empire. Thousands of pilgrims started out to see the wonder, until the roads in summer were white with the pious folk of scrip and staff. Even the sailors on the sea chatted concerning it and the fishermen as they plied their nets, made it the subject of their talk. All agreed that the idol of Kamakura was the biggest thing in earth, air, or ocean.

Now there was a great white Whale living in the Northern Sea who prided himself on being the biggest thing in water and far ahead of any living being on the land.   At first he laughed at the idea that puny men had made an image in their own shape, that could compete with him in size.   He would not believe it, but when he heard of the great pilgrimages and how the coffers of the priests were being filled with the money of the admiring visitors, he was vexed and worried.   Day by day the fleets of ships multiplied on the ocean, sailing right over his head.   They were loaded with people bent on seeing the golden eyes of Buddha.   All the smaller whales and the fish of every fin reported to him that people were talking of nothing else. Every one praised the beauty and extolled the vastness of this greatest wonder in the Everlasting Country of Peaceful Shores.

The big Whale almost went crazy to think of being smaller than an image which men had made.   Fretting and fuming, he thrashed around with his tail, making a great commotion, and rose up to the surface to blow twice as often as usual.   Jealous, indignant, and angry by turns, he seemed a totally different creature from the polite whale of other days. All the fishes gave him a wide berth.   Lonely and miserable, he grew thin with worry. At last, unable to sleep or to eat, he called to him the Shark and questioned him.

"Is it possible that a little man can raise a mountain of copper and make it look like himself?" asked his White Majesty.

"Well, Sire, what one man could not do, thousands of them together might succeed in doing. I myself should like to see the great Buddha they are talking about."

"Go then," said the white Whale, "to the Southern Sea and find out whether this famous idol is as big as I am. Be sure to bring me a true account."

Off started the Shark, and after days and nights of swimming arrived off the shore. Alas, the great image was half a mile inland and sharks cannot walk! He swam around carefully to find some creature with wings or legs to act as his messenger to go and measure the mighty image. Espying a junk lying at anchor near the beach he swam cautiously near. It was a hot day and early in the afternoon, and every man Jack on board was sound asleep, for this was napping time. The Shark soon lost all anxiety concerning harpoons, and fear of having his flesh cut up and put on sale in the fish-shops next day. But what of his messenger?

Happily a Rat, lured out from below decks by the quiet, was running along the low bulwark. It had never been spoken kindly to before and was quite pleased when the Shark—with gentle voice, so as not to arouse the sailors—cried out, as he poked his nose out of the water, "Mr. Rat, I want you to help me. Will you do it?"

The Rat was tickled beyond measure to be thus addressed, and wondered how he could be so useful to so big a fish. He kept back a good distance, however, for he had heard of Cat-fish and did not want to run the risk of being gobbled up. Besides he had listened to the sailors as they talked about people with a "Cat's voice," meaning those who knew how to coax, or flatter. So he was wary.

Then in a low tone the Shark told the Rat what he had come for. It was an honour to serve the lord Whale, as the biggest thing in the world, and it might save his lordship's life, or at least his health, to know the exact facts as to the size of the famous idol.

"Would Mr. Rat be so kind as to go and measure it?" he ended.

"Willingly," said the Rat, feeling highly honored to serve the lord of the ocean and his prime minister.

So, at the first opportunity, the Rat got ashore. He kept his eyes open for fear of Cats, which the Japanese call rat-killers. He ran as fast as he could to the temple which then enclosed the image. Once safely inside, he took his breath, while thinking what next to do.

Truth to tell, the Rat was himself amazed at the size of the image. "A mountain of metal, sure enough," said he. But how should he measure so vast an object? While thinking over the matter, the incense nearly made him sneeze. This he feared to do, lest some Puss should be about and pounce on him. Suddenly a brilliant thought struck him. He walked around the image and counting his steps, found he made five thousand paces. Then he ran back to his home on a junk, crawled down the cable close to the anchor and told the Shark all about what he had seen and gave the measurement.

Heartily thanking his four-legged friend, the Shark was off with a splash that actually woke up the sailors from their naps. One of them ran for a harpoon, but it was too late. Mr. Shark was off. Arriving in that part of the Northern Sea where the Whale was blowing, he told his story. All the reports of the idol's size were true and the circumference of its pedestal was five thousand feet.

Frantic with jealousy and unable to believe the story, the Whale determined to see for himself. Putting on his magic boots, which enabled him to travel overland, he reached the temple at Kamakura at night, when all men were abed, and knocked at the door.

" Come in," sounded the Buddha's voice like the boom of a bell.

" I cannot," groaned the Whale.

" Why not ? "

" Because I am far too large."

" Who are you ?"

" I am the great white Whale of the Northern Sea."

" What do you want ? "

" I want to see if you are bigger than I am. I cannot get in to you, so please come out to me."

Thus respectfully addressed, the idol stepped

off his pedestal, and presented himself outside. The Whale was so overpowered that he trembled and knocked his head on the earth in profound respect. He now believed that what he had heard was almost true. On the other hand, the Buddha was astounded at the Whale's prodigious bulk.

By this time the chief priest and guardian of the temple was awake and up. He was nearly frightened out of his senses to find the pedestal empty. But hearing the conversation, and being invited by both the idol and the Whale to take their measure, he seized his rosary and began to measure. Each watched the other with a jealous eye, but the Whale, to his intense satisfaction, found that he was two inches longer and taller than his rival.

That settled it. Without even once thanking the idol or the priest for the trouble he had given them, he flippered off, slid into the water and was soon spouting in triumph in the great Northern Sea. The idol quietly returned to his pedestal, and as for the priest, when he told his story next day, both his brethren and the people declared it must have been a dream.

Nevertheless the man in the dry-goods store

The Whale found he was two inches longer.

and the dealer in wood and iron settled their
own long standing quarrel as to what was a foot
and agreed to differ.   To this day the " whale
foot " is two inches longer than the " metal
foot."

THE GIFT OF GOLD LACQUER

A THOUSAND years ago the Great Buddha's gospel came to Japan to make the rough people gentle and the cruel kind. Human beings at once began to care for animals. The nobles and common folks alike were glad to hear the good news and learn how to help one another and the dumb brutes.

The Empress ordered that a pagoda should be built in every province and a temple in every village. So happy was every one to see arising in his village so grand a building, that even the boys and girls helped in the work. Some carried stones and wood, others brought clay and plaster. Even the ladies cut off their long black hair and had it made into ropes to haul the materials. The big tree trunks cut in the forest were drawn to the carpenters, who smoothed and shaped them into temple columns.

Soon, in many a village, tall and stately edifices rose high above the thatched cottages of the humble folks. The long sloping roof, instead of being covered with rice straw, was handsomely shingled and the new timber gave out a sweet smell. When the ridge pole was put up the builders set a bow and arrow at each end hoping to shoot and kill any demons that should come near, but they were most afraid of fire that might burn down the building and thus make all their work come to naught. So at the end of the gable they fixed the great devil's tile on which were moulded figures of the water weed to put out the flames. To guard against sparks that might fly out of the chimneys of houses near by, they planted rows of tall trees to act as a wall of defense. Thus they hoped to keep lord Buddha's temple standing for a thousand years.

Then the men that could carve and paint and work metal came up from the capital city to make the inside glorious to behold. Soon the lights and the incense, the shining brass, the burning candles and brilliant altar furniture, the lofty columns made of whole camphor trees, the ceiling of grained wood, the silken rolls of writing on the reading desk, the intoning of the sacred books and the chanting of the priests who were dressed in silk robes, made a splendid sight and a charming sound.

"Isn't it delightful!" said one wrinkled old granny. "I feel quite young again, for I can see and hear and smell as never before."

"Yes, such music and sweet odors and such glory to look upon, I never expected to see," said her daughter, who was a mother and had brought her boy Toko with her.

As for the temple itself, it was full of grown people and children, admiring everything. They felt grateful for the good doctrine taught by the learned priests, some of whom had traveled across the sea from Korea. The first sermon of the bonze was on being kind to all creatures. It was our duty, said he, to love even the worms, and the crickets.

All the beasts of the field and the birds of the air also rejoiced that Buddha's doctrine had come to the Mikado's realm, for now human beings were kinder than ever to their dumb friends with wings or on four feet. Even during the winter, no bird froze or deer starved. Farmers were patient, even with the monkeys that were so numerous as to be mischievous. In the field the white heron could walk unfrightened in the furrows behind the plowman, picking up its food joyfully.

These simple folk were easily pleased, for as yet there was no gilding, or varnish, or fine art, but only plain wood and metal. There was no gold leaf or shining vermilion or violet lacquer yet. Rough and nude enough, the sacred building might seem to a traveler, for it could not compare for a moment with gorgeous temples in India, the gilded ceilings of Korea, or the porcelain pagodas of China.

Happy though they were, yet every one of the villagers wondered how they could make their temple still more lovely. Some even dreamed at night of the far off pagodas, of which their bonze told them. One farmer, who was very kind to the cranes and who carefully refrained from ever killing even an insect, was especially eager to transfer the sheen of the beetles and the gloss of feathers to common wood, and long he pondered on how to do it. He would have the brilliancy of the dragon-fly cover up the knot marks, and the metallic lustre of the pheasant's wings on plain pine. But how to compass the mystery filled him with care.

One night weary with his work in the rice-field, as he slept, a beautiful white bird with black tips on its wing feathers appeared to him and talked about making the tables and altars glossy and rich in color.

"I am the spirit of the lacquer-tree that grows in the deep forest. I poison the men that wound me. My trunk has a milk-white sap. Tap it and stir up the juice in a wooden vessel. Then when it becomes thick, apply it to wood. Then the temple columns will shine like jet. Be wise, and don't laugh when I tell you a secret. It must dry in a wet atmosphere. Guard yourself, for there is danger. Put not your hands in the liquid. Persevere. Be clean. Farewell!"

The farmer woke up and wondered what all this meant, but tired and sleepy his eyes were soon closed again. Not till the raven croaked to tell the sun was risen, did he wake up again. Then remembering the vision, he sallied forth axe in hand with his boy who carried a pail into the forest. Coming to a tree he gave it a blow and out trickled a white juice. It made his nose and eyes tingle, but collecting a pint or so of the stuff, he took it home, and, after agitating it in a platter, left it quiet over night.

The next morning everybody in the house

was growling. Noses, eyes and lips smarted. What was the cause? The now dark fluid was not yet suspected. Another night and their mouths and eyelids felt as if hornets had stung them. On the third day, with their eyes nearly closed, they fumbled about like blind folks. For the first time, they suspected the tree juice, now very black and ugly, and were tempted to throw it away. Nevertheless, though suffering, the farmer lad and father kept their temper and were kinder than ever to the birds in the field.

At night in his dreams the spirit of the tree, in the form of a white crane, again appeared to the farmer.

"Try again and be not discouraged. For your faithfulness in keeping the tree juice, even when you were poisoned, I shall reveal to you another secret, even that of colors and to your son that of gold. This art shall not be born in the fire, like that of the clay which makes cup and vase. I shall show you what water can do. Go forth again. Have more patience."

They obeyed, and this time the father brought also his fair daughter. Behold the three, armed with axe, sap-spout and bucket, going

forth among the bamboo and into the forest.
Selecting a fat trunk, the trio ranged themselves in line a few yards apart.   Then praying
first to the spirit of the tree, and begging
pardon for wounding its body, the man ran
forward and gave a resounding whack which
seemed to stun the tree and make it weep.
Drops fell like tears.   At the same moment
there rose out of the top branches the same
white crane which he had seen in his dream.

The memory of the stinging poisonous sap
made the boy hesitate to rush forward and
insert the spout, so that the sap should not be
wasted.   As if to encourage the lad, the crane
flew down lower and lower and then in circles
round the boy's head.   So plucking up courage,
he dashed up and squeezed the spout into the
gaping wound made by the axe.   Nearly
blinded by the acrid fumes, father and son at a
distance waited to see the girl trip forth bravely
with the bucket.

Only one circling of the encouraging crane
around the maiden's head was necessary to give
her nerve.   In a moment, into the vessel,
which she placed on the ground, the white sap
fell.   Drip, drip, like milk it issued until the

bucket was nearly full, but she and her father and brother kept at a distance.

They waited at home until the stars were out and gone again before approaching the tree again to bring in the twenty-four hours' yield.

" Let us this morning make ourselves pure by cleansing ourselves carefully," said the father, "as the tree spirit said." Fresh from the bath and in clean clothes they sallied forth and brought home their prize.

Night after night the feather-robed spirit of the tree spoke to both father and son in vision, each time commending their faithfulness. Slowly, day by day, the soreness and poisonous effect of the fresh juice, now made into shining lacquer, passed off. They learned to apply it skilfully, clothing common wood with a hard glossy armor. Their wooden bowls, set to dry on shelves sopped with a wet cloth, became like glazed porcelain and their little breakfast table like enamel. Yet the mystery of gloss was not gained in fire but by water. With each opening of the morning glory, the elder gained fresh patience and the younger more skill. Neither heat nor cold, salt or sour hurt lacquer, and common wood seemed like metal. Out of

paper covered with this hard varnish laid on in
many coats, the warriors made coats as tough as
iron.

It was now the boy's turn in his dreams to be
told fresh secrets from the crane. He learned to
mix the varnish with many colors. When he
laid away his work in moisture the lustre became dazzlingly brilliant. One day adding gold
leaf, he found the noble mixture made extra-
ordinary beauty. So still keeping his secret he
traveled to Nara, the capital, and learned drawing and painting from the Korean artists.

Toko now became a decorator of temples and
a maker of altar furniture. He fashioned writing boxes for poetry parties and desks for the
learned monks. On a cabinet of drawers for
his mother he drew and finished in gold lacquer
a picture of his native village and the fields and
hills toward the west. The fame of his skill
reached the ears of the Emperor, who invited
him to make a splendid picnic box, for which
he paid him a thousand rolls of silk. A tray
for the Empress was the wonder of all in the
palace. With gold leaf and lacquer the village
temple now looked like an Imperial shrine. Pilgrims traveled from all over the empire to

admire its splendor and take back home stories of a beauty they had never dreamed of before.

Yet all this time, even when the golden wind-bells, tinkling in the mouths of the phœnixes that hung along the temple eaves, seemed to sing his fame in the evening breezes, did not the artist forget the tree spirit that first told him to be pure and to persevere. But one night in a dream, when sleeping under the old home roof, the silvery white crane again appeared to him, yet this time silent, with no message.

"Speak," said the once farmer lad, now a great master, who had many pupils in art. " How can I express my grateful heart for your kindness to me? I have fame, honor, and wealth, besides the joy of serving the lord Buddha in making his temples beautiful, and the Emperor's palace glorious, besides caring for my old father and mother. What may I do for thee, my guardian spirit?"

" Lord Buddha will ever incline the children of Japan to treat gently the snowy heron and the silk-white cranes forever; but do you and your successors, on the panel, the tray, the screen, and the writing box make the crane and heron comrades of the gold-lacquered mountains and trees, the landscape and the rice-fields. Let them preen their feathers, or soar in the air, or bask in the red disk of the morning sun, or amid the curling spray of the ocean disport themselves in joy. Thus let all the world, for a whole banzai, or a thousand generations, be grateful for the gift of the lacquer tree."

And to this day it is appointed that dull clay can win a glistening robe only in the kiln while the tree juice finds its body in moisture. Shining gold and brilliant colors rise out of the fire, while lacquer owes its richest lustre to the mystery of water. Even yet, alike on the landscape warmed by the sun and on the picture wrought by the artist, the snowy heron steps daintily and the white crane flies to the mountain. So shall it ever be in Everlasting Great Japan.

www.ingramcontent.com/pod-product-compliance
Lightning Source LLC
Chambersburg PA
CBHW072236190626
46809CB00018B/2654

THE ANTIQUARIAN

A BARTON & BROOKS
COSY MYSTERY
BOOK 1

NED HOSTE

Published by Big Ideas Library 2025
Copyright © Ned Hoste, 2025
Ned Hoste has asserted his right to be
identified as the author of this work.

All rights reserved.

This book is sold or supplied subject to the condition
that it shall not, by way of trade or otherwise:

a) be reproduced or copied in whole or in part and in any
form or by any means without the publisher's consent; or

b) be lent, resold, hired out or otherwise circulated
without the publisher's prior consent in any form of
binding or cover other than that in which it is published
and without a similar condition including this condition
being imposed on the subsequent acquirer.

c) No AI training: Without in any way limiting the author's
[and publisher's] exclusive rights under copyright, any use of
this publication to "train" generative artificial intelligence (AI)
technologies to generate text is expressly prohibited. The author
reserves all rights to license uses of this work for generative AI
training and development of machine learning language models.

The moral rights of the author have been asserted.

First published in the United Kingdom in 2025
by Big Ideas Library.
ISBN: 978-1-7384604-6-5

Big Ideas Library
20 Fountayne Street, York YO31 8HL

Design by Ned Hoste
Printed by Mixam (UK)

Big Ideas Library is the publishing division of
The Big Ideas Collective Ltd.